Everyman, I will go with thee,
and be thy guide

Dylan Thomas

THE LOUD HILL
OF WALES
Poetry of Place

Selected and introduced by
WALFORD DAVIES
University of Wales, Aberystwyth

EVERYMAN
J. M. DENT · LONDON
CHARLES E. TUTTLE
VERMONT

J. M. Dent
Orion Publishing Group
Orion House, 5 Upper St Martin's Lane,
London WC2H 9EA
and
Charles E. Tuttle Co., Inc.
28 South Main Street,
Rutland, Vermont 05701, USA

Typeset by Deltatype Ltd, Ellesmere Port
Printed in Great Britain by
The Guernsey Press Co. Ltd, Guernsey, C.I.

British Library Cataloguing-in-Publication Data
is available upon request.

ISBN 0 460 87076 9

CONTENTS

NOTE ON THE AUTHOR AND EDITOR

DYLAN MARLAIS THOMAS was born in Swansea in 1914. After leaving school he worked briefly as a junior reporter on the *South Wales Evening Post* before embarking on a literary career in London. Here he rapidly established himself as one of the finest poets of his generation. *Eighteen Poems* appeared in 1934, *Twenty-five Poems* in 1936, and *Deaths and Entrances* in 1946; his *Collected Poems* was published in 1952. Throughout his life Thomas wrote short stories, his most famous collection being *Portrait of the Artist as a Young Dog*. He also wrote filmscripts, broadcast stories and talks, lectured in America, and wrote the radio play *Under Milk Wood*. In 1953, shortly after his thirty-ninth birthday, he died in New York. His body is buried in Laugharne, Wales, his home for many years.

PROFESSOR WALFORD DAVIES is Director of the Department of Extra-Mural Studies at the University of Wales, Aberystwyth. His previous work on Dylan Thomas includes two critical studies of the poet and the following editions – *Dylan Thomas: Early Prose writings* (1971); *Dylan Thomas: New Critical Essays* (1972); *Dylan Thomas: Selected Poems* (1974); with Ralph Maud, *Dylan Thomas: Collected Poems 1934–1953*. His other publications include editions of the poetry of Wordsworth, Thomas Hardy, and Gerard Manley Hopkins.

INTRODUCTION

A human life, I think, should be well rooted in some spot of a native land, where it may get the love of tender kinship for the face of earth, for the labours men go forth to, for the sounds and accents that haunt it, for whatever will give that early home a familiar unmistakable difference amidst the future widening of knowledge: a spot where the definiteness of early memories may be inwrought with affection, and kindly acquaintance with all neighbours, even to the dogs and donkeys, may spread not by sentimental effort and reflection, but as a sweet habit of the blood. . . . The best introduction to astronomy is to think of the nightly heavens as a little lot of stars belonging to one's own homestead.

(George Eliot, *Daniel Deronda*, ch. 3)

To start an introduction to an anthology representing Dylan Thomas's sense of place with a quotation from George Eliot is to couple two different minds, two different worlds. The obvious 'wisdom' of George Eliot's comment will not immediately (certainly not tonally) bring Dylan Thomas, the 'ring-tailed roarer', to mind. Nevertheless, the George Eliot passage – to which we shall return for points of reference – highlights several central aspects of this sense of belonging to a particular place, a sense which is certainly an important part of the appeal also of Thomas's work.

We can start with one of the obvious differences. George Eliot imagines the celebrated place being the place of one's birth. In that sense, her recommendation that 'a human life . . . should be well rooted in some spot of a native land' has

more in common with, say, Coleridge's prayer for his son in
'Frost at Midnight' (1798) or Yeats's 'A Prayer for My
Daughter' (1919) –

> O may she grow like some green laurel,
> Rooted in one dear perpetual place.

The sense of place is very often mediated in this way, not
only through one's own childhood, but through a prayer for
one's descendants. Thomas's own 'In Country Sleep' (1947;
p. 92), linking Carmarthenshire's rich landscape with the
innocent sleep of his daughter Aeronwy, is in that tradition.
But by the time Philip Larkin, in 'Born Yesterday' (1954),
comes to write his still beautiful inversion of Yeats's poem,
in tribute to Kingsley Amis's daughter –

> In fact, may you be dull –
> If that is what a skilled,
> Vigilant, flexible,
> Unemphasised, enthralled
> Catching of happiness is called –

the idea of rootedness in an originating place has dis-
appeared. A rootedness in one's first place is even more
pointedly cut off in Larkin's similarly inverted version of
Thomas Hood's 'I Remember, I remember, / The house
where I was born'. Naughtily deflating poems such as
Thomas's 'Fern Hill' –

> their farm where I could be
> 'Really myself' –

Larkin in 'I Remember, I Remember' (1954) settles in his
last line for the glum shrug: 'Nothing, like something,
happens anywhere.' Trust Larkin to find the one perfect,
ordinary word to evoke the opposite of what a sense of
place, a sense of somewhere special, means – the word
'anywhere'. That Larkin, too, is one of the great poets of
place ('where sky and Lincolnshire and water meet') does
not disqualify this perfectly healthy demythologization that
stands between us and the Romantics' notion of what

Wordsworth, speaking of childhood, called 'the base on which thy greatness stands'. Indeed, Thomas himself would to some degree be in sympathy with Larkin's sobering correctives. If one wants specifically Wordsworthian 'childhood' and 'landscape' associations from the poetry of place in Thomas's work, one has to start at a very late point in his career. 'The first place poem I've written' is a comment Thomas made about the beautiful birthday piece, 'Poem in October', written as late as 1944. It is a poem prompted directly by that unique and now famous place, Laugharne – and, as such, it inaugurates the specifically scenic poetry of the final phase of the poet's career, from 1944 to 1953.

But the truth is that the often difficult early poetry of the precocious teenager in Swansea, between 1930 and 1934, is also – in deep, if unpastoral, ways – poetry of place. I refer here not only to the excellent 'The hunchback in the park' (p. 63). That is obviously one of the very best possible poems on the literal and imagined places of childhood. And it is significant that its 1932 Swansea draft was the very last poem that Thomas mined from his early poetry notebooks before selling those notebooks to America in 1941. It was a time when he claimed that, under the devastation of German bombs, the Swansea of his childhood (by which he meant his very childhood) had been destroyed. The act of salvaging such an obvious poem of place in the days of holocaust speaks volumes. And in the same way, when in 1938 Thomas wrote several poems about his need to move away from the difficult idiom of his early poetry, in the most central of those poems ('Once it was the colour of saying', p. 74) he rooted his argument about style in the very location in which that early Swansea poetry had been written:

Once it was the colour of saying
Soaked my table the uglier side of a hill
With a capsized field where a school sat still
And a black and white patch of girls grew playing.

In those four lines, we have a brilliantly economic evocation of the teenager at his writing table, looking out over a field. The field is small, 'capsized' – suitably the size of a cap since it contains a school, but also appearing 'capsized' because of the atrocious gradient of Cwmdonkin Drive, the poet's birthplace. We have also that crisp evocation of the imperceptible way in which the black-and-white uniformed schoolgirls seem to grow from few to many when at play on the school field. It is a vignette worthy to stand with Emily Dickinson's embodiment of the passing of time in an equivalent image –

> We passed the School, where Children strove
> At Recess – in the Ring –
> We passed the Fields of Gazing Grain –
> We passed the Setting Sun.

And all this, in Thomas's case, 'the uglier side of a hill' – the other side of which was, not suburban Swansea, but the open countryside that led ultimately to his family's roots in the old Carmarthenshire. The *other* side of that hill would become the source of his later poetry of place, of places such as those commemorated in 'After the funeral', 'Poem in October', 'Fern Hill', and the opening stories of the autobiographical *Portrait of the Artist as a Young Dog*.

But as I say, many of the other early poems, including the ones on dark, elemental themes, had been already suggestive poems of place. The fact that they are poems of urban situation doesn't make them any less 'poems of place', as Thomas Hardy's 'After a Romantic Day' makes clear:

> the blank lack of any charm
> Of landscape did no harm
> The bald steep cutting, rigid, rough
> And moonlit was enough
> For poetry of place.

Why? Because, as Hardy continues, any place or view was for the poet –

> a convenient sheet whereon
> The visions of his mind were drawn.

In any case, we must remember that the milieu and ambience of Dylan Thomas's early poems are not really urban, but *sub*urban. And on the sheet of the visible world as it presented itself to the boy and teenager in the comfortable suburban 'Uplands' of the Swansea of the 1920s and 1930s he drew the visions of an intelligent and imaginative adolescence.

For the teenager, that location was certainly not one in which (in George Eliot's terms) 'the definiteness of early memories may be inwrought with affection, and kindly acquaintance with all neighbours'. Looking out from the safe haven of his terraced home, what the teenager fancied he saw passing his windows was something radically different:

> I see the summer children in their mothers
> Split up the brawned womb's weathers,
> Divide the night and day with fairy thumbs;
> There in the deep with quartered shades
> Of sun and moon they paint their dams
> As sunlight paints the shelling of their heads.
>
> I see that from these boys shall men of nothing
> Stature by seedy shifting . . .

That this vision of unborn children who will grow ('stature') into life-denying adults is bred from an actual view from the windows of No. 5 Cwmdonkin Drive is suggested by a letter to Pamela Hansford Johnson of the same date:

Life passes the windows, and I hate it more minute by minute. I see the rehearsed gestures, the correct smiles, the grey cells revolving around nothing under the godly bowlers. I see the unborn children struggling up the hill in their mothers, beating on the jailing slab of the womb, little realizing what a smugger prison they wish to leap into. . . .

The poetry of place at this stage was very much an

adolescent's revolt against what he saw as 'respectable' society's stifling of the young man's natural appetites and energies. The deft obliqueness with which this poetry of self-assertion is allowed to memorialize, as well as assault, an actual place is one of its attractions. In these lines from 'Do you not father me', the impossibly steep gradient of Cwmdonkin Drive is part of what we have to grasp in order to understand that the poem is a case of the young poet addressing, and challenging, the passers-by:

> Do you not sister me, nor the erected crime
> For my tall turrets carry as your sin?
> Do you not brother me, nor, as you climb,
> Adore my windows for their summer scene?

Much of this early poetry reflects a revolt against the atmosphere and mores of the poet's early world. It is a revolt pungently recorded in 'I have longed to move away' (p. 61):

> I have longed to move away
> From the hissing of the spent lie
> And the old terrors' continual cry
> Growing more terrible as the day
> Goes over the hill into the deep sea. . . .

This repeated image of the hill reminds us of the phrase from another poem by Thomas, the one we have taken as the title of this anthology – 'the loud hill of Wales'. That is the hill of his suburban childhood street, where he first subversively put pen to paper, as well as the sort of image conceived in looking at a relief-map of Wales, with its heavy central spine of mountains:

> Especially when the October wind
> (Some let me make you of autumnal spells,
> The spider-tongued, and the loud hill of Wales)
> With fists of turnips punishes the land . . .
>
> (p. 50)

As such, 'the loud hill of Wales' represents something

different – and ultimately more internal – from Gerard Manley Hopkins's externally friendly phrase, 'this world of Wales'. The synaesthesic 'loudness' and 'spider-tongued' quality of Thomas's hill remind us of the fact that it is home to a poet and noisy maker of words – and a home that was, like Wales itself, at the *lowest* estimate, *bi*lingual. But the adjectives also suggest the very urge he felt to explode, and explode out of, his frustrated sense of belonging.

But we have to recognize, along with his dramatised longing 'to move away', his realization that this is also where he incorrigibly belongs. His deep sense of *belonging* to suburban Swansea is stated even in the poem 'I have longed to move away' itself:

> I have longed to move away but am afraid. . . .

And it is stressed further in a 1936 letter to his poet-friend Vernon Watkins from the large 'out-of-doors' in Cornwall:

here the out-of-doors is very beautiful, but it's a strange country to me, all scenery and landscape, and I'd rather the bound slope of a suburban hill, the Elms, the Acacias, Rookery Nook, Curlew Avenue. . . . I stand for, if anything, the aspidistra, the provincial drive, the morning cafe, the evening pub. . . .

Even so, those preposterously unrealistic names for suburban houses remind us that, beneath it all, desire for the rural runs. Thomas's repeated celebrations of Cwmdonkin Park are therefore in many ways a town-boy's frustrated pastorialism, and the unpublished Notebook poem 'Rain cuts the place we tread' (p. 16) shows nature's expanse and excitement being mimed even on garden paths: 'We sail a boat upon the path, / Paddle with leaves / Down an ecstatic line of light . . .'. This childlike ability to transcend the merely domestic or merely civic sense of place is evoked also in the prose. In the short story 'The Tree', for example, the boy enacts a voyage fantasy:

The house changed to his moods, and a lawn was the sea or the shore or the sky or whatever he wished it. When a lawn was a sad mile of water, and he was sailing on a broken flower down the waves, the gardener would come out of his shed near the island of bushes. He too would take a stalk and sail.

It was essentially in the miniature Eden of the home garden or the suburban park that Thomas first tasted what we saw George Eliot describe as 'the love of tender kinship for the face of earth'. It was probably these town-boy beginnings that sharpened the poet's appetite in his later celebrations of Fern Hill (p. 85) and Sir John's Hill (p. 96). That is why I have prefaced those major Carmarthenshire poems with the mere verse of 'The Countryman's Return' (p. 69), a piece of loose-limbed satire which reminds us that Swansea's young dog had also been a young lion in London in the years preceding his first settlement at Laugharne in 1938.

But we must not forget that the 'suburban' itself, and the tension between it and the 'rural', produced a poetry of tremendously characterful power. The poem from which the title of this anthology is taken – 'Especially when the October wind' (p. 49) – is a major expression of the 'Rimbaud of Cwmdonkin Drive''s vision of himself as a poet caught between domesticity and wildness, between words and things:

> Shut, too, in a tower of words, I mark
> On the horizon walking like the trees
> The wordy shapes of women, and the rows
> Of the star-gestured children in the park. . . .

> Behind a pot of ferns the wagging clock
> Tells me the hour's word, the neural meaning
> Flies on the shafted disk. . . .

At the same time, we must not forget that this wonderful sense of a suburban place gave him also images to celebrate his agreement with Keats, that one should modestly expect 'only a gradual ripening of the intellectual powers'. What Keats further described as an ability to 'remain in a state of half knowledge, without an irritable reaching after fact and reason' is what is celebrated in Thomas's 'Why east wind chills' (p. 58) and 'Should lanterns shine' (p. 60), with its poignant close:

> The ball I threw while playing in the park
> Has not yet reached the ground.

How wise of Thomas's Swansea poet-friend, Vernon Watkins, to advise him to cut out the two lines that had originally followed that fine ending. By adding 'Regard the moon, it hangs above the lawn; / Regard the lawn, it lies beneath the moon' Thomas had originally merely imitated T. S. Eliot and Laforgue. If he was aiming to emulate T. S. Eliot's sense of place, he had already more effectively done so in 'That sanity be kept' (p. 28), which is a fine suburban version of Eliot's urban 'Morning at the Window'.

These early poems are very much caught up in their sense of the poet's own self. The middle and later phases of his short career show an admirable emergence into a more varied, external, objective world. A major poem such as 'After the funeral' (p. 72), which is an elegy on the death of the 'peasant aunt' Ann Jones who had presided over the Swansea schoolboy's now famous holidays at Fern Hill, seeks to set him back in warmer relationship to the Welsh puritanical roots he had earlier revolted against. Just as we saw him call 'Poem in October' the 'first place poem I've written', in 1949 he described 'After the funeral' (1938) as 'the only one I have written that is, directly, about the life and death of one particular human being I knew'. Its location is the Fern Hill farm, but the degree to which its focus is a person, rather than a place, offers an interesting contrast to the poem 'Fern Hill' itself. At the same time, both poems contrast markedly with the more straight-forward realism of the treatment of the same farm in 'The Peaches', the opening story of *Portrait of the Artist as a Young Dog*. Nevertheless, 'After the funeral' is the first poem to root Thomas's imagination in the Carmarthenshire landscape that was to prove the deepest life of his later poetry. In the same year (1938), a strong sense of landscape could inform even a poem that now carries no sign of it.

When in 1938 Thomas was working on 'On no work of
words' – a pained lament on the absence of inspiration and
creativity – its first stanza, later jettisoned, read:

> For three lean months now, no work done
> In summer Laugharne among the cockle boats
> And by the castle with the boatlike birds.

This was the last case in which a sense of place, strongly
informing the first drafts of a poem, was subsequently
allowed to fade from the final poem itself. From 1938
onwards, place and landscape, if relevant to a poem's first
inspiration, were here to stay.

The Second World War ultimately drove Thomas back to
London in search of profitable employment of his broad-
casting and filmscripting talents. There, amidst the
bombing raids that were at the same time demolishing the
Swansea of his childhood, he wrote relatively little poetry.
But his poems about the victims of that war were powerful
celebrations of life in the face of obscene death. And the
complete range of his work from 1944/45 onwards,
wonderfully evocative of landscape and often of childhood,
stands over against a sense of outrage that man's in-
humanity to man (in the form of the war and the advent of
the nuclear age), even more than neutral Time, destroys our
sense of pattern and permanence in the world. The later
poems in this volume are therefore not idly descriptive, and
what the exerpts from *Under Milk Wood* evoke is not mere
quaintness. In Thomas's own phrase about Llareggub, they
are meditations on – and celebrations of – 'a place of love'.
This is so, even though the poems themselves evoke
landscapes emblematic of decay and experience as much as
of growth and innocence. George Eliot's 'dogs and donkeys'
are replaced by Thomas's dolphins, seals, cormorants,
herons and hawks. The centrality of a sense of 'place' is
emphasized by Thomas's own description of his vantage-
point, the now famous writing-shed near the Boathouse at
Laugharne, his 'house on stilts high among beaks / And
palavers of birds', looking out over the beautiful estuary of

two rivers, and across to Sir John's Hill. It is now a view (and a point of view) very different from that afforded by the window overlooking the steep road outside Cwmdonkin Drive.

But it would be a mistake to imagine that Thomas belonged to Laugharne in deeper ways than to his native Swansea. He belonged to the two places in essentially different ways. Swansea was the beginning place. There, a high intelligence and a burning talent had to be scored into the fences of the no-go areas dictated by the society of his parents and elders, and into the shields fending off the 'provincial' from the praise of literary London. The achievement of Thomas's early poetry is its distillation, for his generation, of a Blakean spirit of revolt. In the later poetry at Laugharne, we have the greatly lionized poet, ultimately with America beckoning, contemplating land-scapes that linked him more and more to the mainstream of poetry stemming from Vaughan and Wordsworth. It was still a beginning place, but more now in the mythic, Edenic sense. But it also genuinely rooted him, affectionately, 'in one dear perpetual place'. To quote thus from the Irish Yeats is appropriate, because all this was still in *Wales*, not England. Thomas stated categorically more than once that it was only in Wales that he could write.

The George Eliot quotation with which we started claims that 'the best introduction to astronomy is to think of the nightly heavens as a little lot of stars belonging to one's own homestead'. As it happens, it is at least legally true that we have rights in the air above us and in the land beneath our feet. But William Empson's poem 'Legal Fiction' wittily takes that quaint notion of real-estate to stunning con-clusions:

> Your rights extend under and above your claim
> Without bound; you own land in Heaven and Hell;
> Your part of earth's surface and mass the same,
> Of all cosmos' volume, and all stars as well.

Man's reallest estate is that in which he knows that he does *not* own any part of the world. Thomas's importance as a poet resides greatly in the seriousness with which he explored in his poems the individual's mysterious relationship – sometimes reassuring, sometimes daunting – to the physical world around him. The quaintness of George Eliot's remark above, from a novel, should be placed next to her deeper comment in a letter:

I try to delight on the sunshine that will be when I shall never see it any more. And I think it is possible for this sort of impersonal life to attain great intensity – possible for us to gain much more independence, than is usually believed, of the small bundle of facts that make our own personality.

That is the kind of wisdom feeding late Thomas poems such as 'Over Sir John's hill' (p. 96) and 'Poem on his Birthday' (p. 98). One of the repeated powers in the poetry, early and late, is that of sensing Eden in all that lies about us:

So it must have been after the birth of the simple light
In the first spinning place. . . .

But it is never pictured as an Eden that excludes the Fall, or ignores Time, or survives cynicism. If I may borrow words from a poem by Ken Gransden, Thomas's poetry often talks of a first place but always remembers that 'it was not the first place'. The Dylan Thomas who celebrates the landscapes of his late poems can also be thought of as daily learning the lesson with which the same Ken Gransden poem ends:

Try and grow used to the place of every star,
And forget your own dark house.

WALFORD DAVIES

I

'I trumpet the place,
From fish to jumping hill . . .'

Prologue

This day winding down now
At God speeded summer's end
In the torrent salmon sun,
In my seashaken house
On a breakneck of rocks
Tangled with chirrup and fruit,
Froth, flute, fin and quill
At a wood's dancing hoof,
By scummed, starfish sands
With their fishwife cross
Gulls, pipers, cockles, and sails,
Out there, crow black, men
Tackled with clouds, who kneel
To the sunset nets,
Geese nearly in heaven, boys
Stabbing, and herons, and shells
That speak seven seas,
External waters away
From the cities of nine
Days' night whose towers will catch
In the religious wind
Like stalks of tall, dry straw,
At poor peace I sing
To you, strangers, (though song
Is a burning and crested act,
The fire of birds in
The world's turning wood,
For my sawn, splay sounds),
Out of these seathumbed leaves
That will fly and fall
Like leaves of trees and as soon
Crumble and undie
Into the dogdayed night.
Seaward the salmon, sucked sun slips,
And the dumb swans drub blue

My dabbed bay's dusk, as I hack
This rumpus of shapes
For you to know
How I, a spinning man,
Glory also this star, bird
Roared, sea born, man torn, blood blest.
Hark: I trumpet the place,
From fish to jumping hill! Look:
I build my bellowing ark
To the best of my love
As the flood begins,
Out of the fountainhead
Of fear, rage red, manalive,
Molten and mountainous to stream
Over the wound asleep
Sheep white hollow farms

To Wales in my arms.
Hoo, there, in castle keep,
You king singsong owls, who moonbeam
The flickering runs and dive
The dingle furred deer dead!
Huloo, on plumbed bryns,
O my ruffled ring dove
In the hooting, nearly dark
With Welsh and reverent rook,
Coo rooing the woods' praise,
Who moons her blue notes from her nest
Down to the curlew herd!
Ho, hullaballoing clan
Agape, with woe
In your beaks, on the gabbing capes!
Heigh, on horseback hill, jack
Whisking hare! who
Hears, there, this fox light, my flood ship's
Clangour as I hew and smite
(A clash of anvils for my

Hubbub and fiddle, this tune
On a tongued puffball)
But animals thick as thieves
On God's rough tumbling grounds
(Hail to His beasthood!).
Beasts who sleep good and thin,
Hist, in hogsback woods! The haystacked
Hollow farms in a throng
Of waters cluck and cling,
And barnroofs cockcrow war!
O kingdom of neighbours, finned
Felled and quilled, flash to my patch
Work ark and the moonshine
Drinking Noah of the bay,
With pelt, and scale, and fleece:
Only the drowned deep bells
Of sheep and churches noise
Poor peace as the sun sets
And dark shoals every holy field.
We shall ride out alone, and then,
Under the stars of Wales,
Cry, Multitudes of arks! Across
The water lidded lands,
Manned with their loves they'll move,
Like wooden islands, hill to hill.
Huloo, my prowed dove with a flute!
Ahoy, old, sea-legged fox,
Tom tit and Dai mouse!
My ark sings in the sun
At God speeded summer's end
And the flood flowers now.

II

'This sea town was my world . . .'

Reminiscences of Childhood (*First Version*)

I was born in a large Welsh industrial town at the beginning of the Great War: an ugly, lovely town (or so it was, and is, to me), crawling, sprawling, slummed, unplanned, jerry-villa'd, and smug-suburbed by the side of a long and splendid-curving shore where truant boys and sandfield boys and old anonymous men, in the tatters and hangovers of a hundred charity suits, beachcombed, idled, and paddled, watched the dock-bound boats, threw stones into the sea for the barking, outcast dogs, and, on Saturday summer afternoons, listened to the militant music of salvation and hell-fire preached from a soap-box.

This sea town was my world; outside, a *strange* Wales, coal-pitted, mountained, river run, full, so far as I knew, of choirs and sheep and story-book tall hats, moved about its business which was none of mine; beyond that unknown Wales lay England, which was London, and a country called 'The Front' from which many of our neighbours never came back. At the beginning, the only 'front' I knew was the little lobby before our front door; I could not understand how so many people never returned from there; but later I grew to know more, though still without understanding, and carried a wooden rifle in Cwmdonkin Park and shot down the invisible, unknown enemy like a flock of wild birds. And the park itself was a world within the world of the sea town; quite near where I lived, so near that on summer evenings I could listen, in my bed, to the voices of other children playing ball on the sloping, paper-littered bank; the park was full of terrors and treasures. The face of one old man who sat, summer and winter, on the same bench looking over the swanned reservoir, I can see more clearly than the city-street faces I saw an *hour* ago: and years later I wrote a poem about, and for, this never, by me, to-be-forgotten 'Hunchback in the Park'. . . .[1]

[1] See below, p. 63.

And that park grew up with me; that small, interior world widened as I learned its names and its boundaries; as I discovered new refuges and ambushes in its miniature woods and jungles, hidden homes and lairs for the multitudes of the young, for cowboys and Indians and, most sinister of all, for the far-off race of the Mormons, a people who every night rode on nightmares through my bedroom. In that small, iron-railed universe of rockery, gravel-path, playbank, bowling-green, bandstand, reservoir, chrysanthemum garden, where an ancient keeper known as Smoky was the tyrannous and whiskered snake in the grass one must keep off, I endured, with pleasure, the first agonies of unrequited love, the first slow boiling in the belly of a bad, poem, the strutting and raven-locked self-dramatization of what, at the time, seemed incurable adolescence. I wrote then, in a poem never to be published:

> See, on gravel paths under the harpstrung trees,
> Feeling the summer wind, hearing the swans,
> Leaning from windows over a length of lawns,
> On tumbling hills admiring the sea,
> I am alone, alone complain to the stars.
> Who are his friends? The wind is his friend,
> The glow-worm lights his darkness, and
> The snail tells of coming rain.[1]

But several years even before those lines, I had written:

Where could I ever listen for the sound of seas asleep,
Or the cold and graceful song of a swan that dies and wakes,
Where could I ever hear the cypress speak in its sleep,
And cling to a manhood of flowers, and sing the
    unapproachable lakes?

I am afraid the answer was, the park. (I had 'the swan' on the brain in those days; luckily, there were very few rhymes for 'parrot.') The answer was, the park; a bit of bush and flowerbed and lawn in a snug, smug, trim, middling-

---

[1] See below, p. 63.

prosperous suburb of my utterly confining outer world, that splendidly ugly sea town where, with my friends, I used to dawdle on half-holidays along the bent and Devon-facing seashore, hoping for corpses or gold watches or the skull of a sheep or a message in a bottle to be washed up in the wrack; or where we used to wander, whistling and being rude to strangers, through the packed streets, stale as station sandwiches, around the impressive gas-works and the slaughter-house, past the blackened monuments of civic pride and the museum, which should have been in a museum; where we scratched at a kind of cricket on the bald and cindery surface of the recreation-ground, or winked at unapproachably old girls of fifteen or sixteen on the promenade opposite; where we took a tram that shook like an iron jelly down from our neat homes to the gaunt pier, there to clamber *under* the pier, hanging perilously on its skeleton-legs; or to run along to the end where patient men with the seaward eyes of the dockside unemployed, capped and mufflered, dangling from their mouths pipes that had long gone out, angled over the edge for unpleasant tasting fish. Never *was* there such a town as ours, I thought, as we fought on the sandhills with the boys that our mothers called 'common,' or dared each other up the scaffolding of half-built houses, soon to be called Laburnums or the Beeches, near the residential districts where the solider business families 'dined' at half past seven and never drew the curtains. Never *was* there such a town (I thought) for the smell of fish and chips on Saturday nights; for the Saturday afternoon cinema matinées where we shouted and hissed our threepences away; for the crowds in the streets, with leeks in their pockets, on international nights, for the singing that gushed from the smoky doorways of the pubs in the quarters we never should have visited; for the park, the inexhaustibly ridiculous and mysterious, the bushy Red-Indian-hiding park, where the hunchback sat alone, images of perfection in his head, and 'the groves were blue with sailors.'

The recollections of childhood have no order; of all those

every-coloured and shifting scented shoals that move below the surface of the moment of recollection, one, two, indiscriminately, suddenly, dart up out of their revolving waters into the present air: immortal flying-fish.

So I remember that never was there such a dame-school as ours: so firm and kind and smelling of galoshes, with the sweet and fumbled music of the piano-lessons drifting down from upstairs to the lonely schoolroom where only the sometimes tearful wicked sat over undone sums or to repent a little crime, the pulling of a girl's hair during geography, the sly shin-kick under the table during prayers. Behind the school was a narrow lane where the oldest and boldest threw pebbles at windows, scuffled and boasted, lied about their relations –

'My father's got a chauffeur.'
'What's he want a chauffeur for, he hasn't got a car.'
'My father's the richest man in Swansea.'
'My father's the richest man in Wales.'
'My father's the richest man in the world' –
and smoked the butt-ends of cigarettes, turned green, went home, and had little appetite for tea.

The lane was the place to tell your secrets; if you did not have any, you invented them; I had few. Occasionally, now, I dream that I am turning, after school, into the lane of confidences where I say to the children of my class: 'At last I have a secret.'

'What is it? What is it?'

'I can fly!' And when they do not believe me, I flap my arms like a large, stout bird and slowly leave the ground, only a few inches at first, then gaining air until I fly, like Dracula in a schoolboy cap, level with the windows of the school, peering in until the mistress at the piano screams, and the metronome falls with a clout to the ground, stops, and there is no more Time; and I fly over the trees and chimneys of my town, over the dockyards, skimming the masts and funnels; over Inkerman Street and Sebastopol Street and the street of the man-capped women hurrying to the Jug and Bottle with a fish-frail full of empties; over the trees of the eternal park, where a brass band shakes the leaves and sends them showering down on to the nurses and the children, the cripples and the out-of-work. This is only a dream. The ugly, lovely, at least to me, town is alive, exciting and real though war has made a hideous hole in it. I do not need to remember a dream. The reality is there. The fine, live people, the spirit of Wales itself.

The corn blows from side to side

The corn blows from side to side lightly,
Tenuous, yellow forest that it is,
And bears the steady wind on its head,
Brushing my two hands.
The flower, under the soil
Rounds its ungainly roots;
Blue flower,
In my continent of strange speech,
Divide and allow the path
Of my warm arm to touch you,
Then touch you again
Not with the drift of voluptuous fingers
But with the possession
That comes from obscure contact.
I must shape the corn
Into a phalanx that satisfies
The eye watching it move,
Mould and round and make mine;
Your tall, straight stalks
Inclining only to the heaviest wind,
Will be my architecture
And my pride above the flower
Whose roots I cannot feel;
I will mount you upon resolute love;
I will raise your columns.
Now flower,
Traveller through the earth,

Spiral and pleasant to the extent
Of your violent, blue way,
Shall I make more of you
Than the ghost from the grave?
Shall I turn you and better you
As I bettered the yellow corn
From one architecture to another?
You move in your island
Like a dark cloud high above the ground,
You circle your stalk
On the night sailing with care and skill.
I know your roots thrust fine, black teeth
Up into the soil,
And swell noiselessly.
In the spire of the top petal
Rings the loud bell of triumph,
As you arch and become longer.
My influence breaks your spell,
And now you can grow,
Now you can cut and hurt the cloud,
Giant-flower.

The hill of sea and sky is carried

The hill of sea and sky is carried
High on the sounding wave,
To float, an island in its size,
And stem the waters of the sun
Which fall and fall.
Wind cannot spin the cloth
Of safety with such care,
Lacing the water and the air together;
Nor hail, nor season, weave
A hill like that.
Only the water loads its garden

With rich and airy soil,
Heaps on the paths the broken clouds,
And arches his long wave.
He is to plough the air,
Plough up and turn the sweet, blue fields,
And wrench the flowers by their roots;
He'll be at liberty
To plant what curious seeds he knows
When this is done.

Admit the sun

Admit the sun into your high nest
Where the eagle is a strong bird
And where the light comes cautiously
To find and then to strike;
Let the frost harden
And the shining rain
Drop onto your wings,
Bruising the tired feathers.

I build a fortress from a heap of flowers;
Wisdom is stored with the clove
And the head of the bright poppy.
I bury, I travel to find pride
In the age of Lady Frankincense
Lifting her smell over the city buildings.
Where is there greater love
For the muscular and the victorious
Than in the gull and the fierce eagle
Who do not break?

Take heed of strength!
It is a weapon that can turn back

From the well-made hand
Out of the air it strikes.

Here is the bright green sea

Here is the bright green sea,
And, underneath, a thousand fishes
Moving their scaly bodies soundlessly
Among a bright green world of weeds.
These thousand pebbles are a thousand eyes
Each sharper than the sun;
These waves are dancers;
Upon a thousand, pointed toes
They step the sea,
Lightly, as in a pantomime.

My golden bird the sun

My golden bird the sun
Has spread his wings and flown away
Out of the swinging cage
You call the sky,
And, like his tired shadow
White with love,
My silver bird the moon
Flies up again
Onto her perch of stars.

Rain cuts the place we tread

Rain cuts the place we tread,
A sparkling fountain for us

With no fountain boy but me
To balance on my palms
The water from a street of clouds.
We sail a boat upon the path,
Paddle with leaves
Down an ecstatic line of light,
Watching, not too aware
To make our senses take too much,
The unrolled waves
So starred with gravel,
The living vessels of the garden
Drifting in easy time;
And, as we watch, the rainbow's foot
Stamps on the ground,
A legendary horse with hoof and feather,
Impatient to be off.
He goes across the sky,
But, when he's out of sight,
The mark his flying tail has left
Branches a million shades,
A gay parabola
Above a boat of leaves and weeds.
We try to steer;
The stream's fantastically hard,
Too stiff to churn with leaves,
A sedge of broken stalks and shells.
This is a drain of iron plants,
For when we touch a flower with our oar
We strike but do not stir it.
Our boat is made to rise
By waves which grow again
Their own melodious height,
Into the rainbow's shy embrace.
We shiver uncomplainingly,
And taste upon our lips, this minute,
The emerald caress,
And breath on breath of indigo.

The morning, space for Leda

The morning, space for Leda
To stir the water with a buoyant foot,
And interlude for violins
To catch her sailing down the stream –
The phrases on the wood aren't hers;
A fishing bird has notes of ivory
Alive within his craning throat –
Sees the moon still up,
Bright, well-held head,
And, for a pivot,
The shadows from the glassy sea
To wet the sky with tears,
And daub the unrisen sun with longing.
The swan makes strings of water in her wake;
Between the moon and sun
There's time to pluck a tune upon the harp,
Moisten the mouth of sleep
To kiss awake
My hand with honey that had closed upon a flower.
Between the rising and the falling
Spring may be green –
Under her cloth of trees no sorrow,
Under her grassy dress no limbs –
And winter follow like an echo
The summer voice so warm from fruit
That clustered round her shoulders,
And hid her uncovered breast.
The morning, too, is time for love,
When Leda, on a toe of down,
Dances invisibly, a swan to see
Who holds her clasped inside his strong, white wings;
And darkness, hand in hand with light,
Is blind with tears too frail to taste.

Yesterday, the cherry sun

Yesterday, the cherry sun
Hung in its space until the steel string snapped,
The voice lost edge,
And the guitar was put away,
Dropping from the window
Into the paper sea,
A silver dog, a gypsy's hoop.
The handle's turned this time;
The sun again, you pretty fruit,
I almost touch it, press you, vein for vein,
But other tunes meet mine,
Turned by the handles,
Suave on their chiming stilts.
Your serenade upon machines,
The fifty discs that soar to you
In notes like stone-made circles
Growing larger, tick by tick,
Should make you glad;
Your face is pale,
And when I catch your rays
Upon the garden fork,
The beds aren't bathed with light,
And the crocus does not cry for shade.
The handle and the clockwork turn,
But the nightingale
Does not please the emperor;
I pluck again
The sweet, steel strings
To bring the sun to life,
Laugh at the echo made,
The steel bird put away,
Guitar in hand.

Since, on a quiet night, I heard them talk

Since, on a quiet night, I heard them talk
Who have no voices but the winds'
Of all the mystery there is in life
And all the mastery there is in death,
I have not lain an hour asleep
But troubled by their curious speech
Stealing so softly into the ears.
One says: There was a woman with no friend,
And, standing over the sea, she'd cry
Her loneliness across the empty waves
Time after time.
And every voice:
Oblivion is as loverless;
Oblivion is as loverless.
And then again: There was a child
Upon the earth who knew no joy,
For there was no light in his eyes,
And there was no light in his soul.
Oblivion is as blind,
Oblivion is as blind,
I hear them say out of the darkness
Who have no talk but that of death.

Written for a Personal Epitaph

Feeding the worm
Who do I blame
Because laid down
At last by time,
Here under the earth with girl and thief,
Who do I blame?
Mother I blame
Whose loving crime

Moulded my form
Within her womb,
Who gave me life and then the grave,
Mother I blame.
Here is her labour's end,
Dead limb and mind,
All love and sweat
Gone now to rot.
I am man's reply to every question,
His aim and destination.

Take up this seed

Take up this seed, it is most beautiful,
Within its husk opening in fire and air
Into a flower's stem and a flower's mouth,
To lean upon the wall of summer
And touch the lips of the dark wind.
Lift up this seed; life from its circle
Spins towards light,
Full-voiced from many seasons' sounds
And, in a fruit's fall or a bird's fall,
Is one with all plants in the earth's well,
Such is its miracle.
Touch these broad leaves, all fiery-veined,
Touch these green leaves and this fair stalk;
Fair as they are the seed is fairer,
Budding to light out of its own darkness;
What once was hot beneath the earth's as cool as rain,
As sweet as rain, as falling soft as snow;
What lay unknowing in the soil
Of any weariness at all
Now droops and sleeps at the day's end,
And at its hour's end lets death be friend and comforter.

What once was beautiful is dead,
Was sweet is sour.

Being but men, we walked into the trees

Being but men, we walked into the trees
Afraid, letting our syllables be soft
For fear of waking the rooks,
For fear of coming
Noiselessly into a world of wings and cries.

If we were children we might climb,
Catch the rooks sleeping, and break no twig,
And, after the soft ascent,
Thrust out our heads above the branches
To wonder at the unfailing stars.

Out of confusion, as the way is,
And the wonder that man knows,
Out of the chaos would come bliss.

That, then, is loveliness, we said,
Children in wonder watching the stars,
Is the aim and the end.

Being but men we walked into the trees.

Nearly summer

Nearly summer, and the devil
Still comes visiting his poor relations,
If not in person sends his unending evil

By messengers, the flight of birds
Spelling across the sky his devil's news,
The seasons' cries, full of his intimations.
He has the whole field now, the gods departed
Who cannot count the seeds he sows,
The law allows,
His wild carouses, and his lips
Pursed at the ready ear
To whisper, when he wants, the senses' war
Or lay the senses' rumour.
The welcome devil comes as guest,
Steals what is best – the body's splendour –
Rapes, leaves for lost (the amorist!),
Counts on his fist
All he has reaped in wonder.

The welcome devil comes invited,
Suspicious but that soon passes.
They cry to be taken, and the devil breaks
All that is not already broken,
Leaves it among the cigarette ends and the glasses.

Walking in gardens

Walking in gardens by the sides
Of marble bathers toeing the garden ponds,
Skirting the ordered beds of paint-box flowers,
We spoke of drink and girls, for hours
Touched on the outskirts of the mind,
Then stirred a little chaos in the sun.
A new divinity, a god of wheels
Destroying souls and laying waste,
Trampling to dust the bits and pieces
Of faulty men and their diseases,
Rose in our outworn brains. We spoke our lines,

Made, for the bathers to admire,
Dramatic gestures in the air.
Ruin and revolution
Whirled in our words, then faded.
We might have tried light matches in the wind.
Over and round the ordered garden hummed,
There was no need of a new divinity,
No tidy flower moved, no bather gracefully
Lifted her marble foot, or lowered her hand
To brush upon the waters of the pond.

Before the gas fades

Before the gas fades with a harsh last bubble,
And the hunt in the hatstand discovers no coppers,
Before the last fag and the shirt sleeves and slippers,
The century's trap will have snapped round your middle,
Before the allotment is weeded and sown,
And the oakum is picked, and the spring trees have grown
                                                    green,
And the state falls to bits,
And is fed to the cats,
Before civilization rises or rots
(It's a matter of guts,
Graft, poison, and bluff,
Sobstuff, mock reason,
The chameleon coats of the big bugs and shots),
The jaws will have shut, and life be switched out.
Before the arrival of angel or devil,
Before evil or good, light or dark,
Before white or black, the right or left sock,
Before good or bad luck.

Man's manmade sparetime lasts the four seasons,
Is empty in springtime, and no other time lessens

The bitter, the wicked, the longlying leisure,
Sleep punctured by waking, dreams
Broken by choking,
The hunger of living, the oven and gun
That turned on and lifted in anger
Make the hunger for living
When the purse is empty
And the belly is empty,
The harder to bear and the stronger.
The century's trap will have closed for good
About you, flesh will perish, and blood
Run down the world's gutters,
Before the world steadies, stops rocking, is steady,
Or rocks, swings and rocks, before the world totters.

Caught in the trap's machinery, lights out,
With sightless eyes and hearts that do not beat,
You will not see the steadying or falling,
Under the heavy layers of the night
Not black or white or left or right.

We who were young are old

'We who were young are old. It is the oldest cry.
Age sours before youth's tasted in the mouth
And any sweetness that it hath
Is sucked away'.

We who are still young are old. It is a dead cry,
The squeal of the damned out of the old pit.
We have grown weak before we could grow strong,
For us there is no shooting and no riding,
The Western man has lost one lung,
And cannot mount a clotheshorse without bleeding.

Until the whisper of the last trump louden
We shall play Chopin in our summer garden,
With half-averted heads, as if to listen,
Play Patience in the parlour after dark.
For us there is no riding and no shooting,
No frosty gallops through the winter park.
We who are young sit holding yellow hands
Before the fire, and hearken to the wind.

No faith to fix the teeth on carries
Men old before their time into dark valleys
Where death lies dead asleep, one bright eye open,
No faith to sharpen the old wits leaves us
Lost in the shades, no course, no use
To fight through the invisible weeds,
No faith to follow is the world's curse
That falls on chaos.

There is but one message for the earth,
Young men with fallen chests and old men's breath,
Women with cancer at their sides
And cancerous speaking dripping from their mouths,
And lovers turning on the gas,
Exsoldiers with horrors for a face,
A pig's snout for a nose,
The lost in doubt, the nearly mad, the young
Who, undeserving, have suffered the earth's wrong,
The living dead left over from the war,
The living after, the filled with fear,
The caught in the cage, the broken winged,
The flying loose, albino eyed, wing singed,
The white, the black, the yellow and mulatto
From Harlem, Bedlam, Babel, and the Ghetto,
The Piccadilly men, the back street drunks,
The grafters of cats' heads on chickens' trunks,
The whole, the crippled, the weak and strong,
The Western man with one lung gone –
Faith fixed beyond the spinning stars,

Fixed faith, believing and worshipping together
In god or gods, christ or his father,
Mary, virgin, or any other.
Faith. Faith. Firm faith in many or one,
Faith fixed like a star beyond the stars,
And the skysigns and the night lights,
And the shores of the last sun.

We who are young are old, and unbelieving,
Sit at our hearths from morning until evening,
Warming dry hands and listening to the air;
We have no faith to set between our teeth.
Believe, believe and be saved, we cry, who have no faith.

Out of a war of wits

Out of a war of wits, when folly of words
Was the world's to me, and syllables
Fell hard as whips on an old wound,
My brain came crying into the fresh light,
Called for confessor but there was none
To purge after the wits' fight,
And I was struck dumb by the sun.
Praise that my body be whole, I've limbs,
Not stumps, after the hour of battle,
For the body's brittle and the skin's white.
Praise that only the wits are hurt after the wits' fight.
The sun shines strong, dispels
Where men are men men's smells.
Overwhelmed by the sun, with a torn brain
I stand beneath the clouds' confessional,
But the hot beams rob me of speech,
After the perils of fools' talk
Reach asking arms up to the milky sky,
After a volley of questions and replies
Lift wit-hurt head for sun to sympathize,

And the sun heals, closing sore eyes.
It is good that the sun shine,
And, after it has sunk, the sane moon,
For out of a house of matchboard and stone
Where men would argue till the stars be green,
It is good to step onto the earth, alone,
And be struck dumb, if only for a time.

Their faces shone under some radiance

Their faces shone under some radiance
Of mingled moonlight and lamplight
That turned the empty kisses into meaning,
The island of such penny love
Into a costly country, the graves
That neighboured them to wells of warmth
(And skeletons had sap). One minute
Their faces shone; the midnight rain
Hung pointed in the wind,
Before the moon shifted and the sap ran out,
She, in her summer frock, saying some cheap thing,
And he replying,
Not knowing radiance came and passed.
The suicides parade again, now ripe for dying.

That sanity be kept

That sanity be kept I sit at open windows,
Regard the sky, make unobtrusive comment on the moon,
Sit at open windows in my shirt,
And let the traffic pass, the signals shine,
The engines run, the brass bands keep in tune,
For sanity must be preserved.

Thinking of death, I sit and watch the park
Where children play in all their innocence,
And matrons, on the littered grass,
Absorb the daily sun.

The sweet suburban music from a hundred lawns
Comes softly to my ears. The English mowers mow and
mow.

I mark the couples walking arm in arm,
Observe their smiles,
Sweet invitations and inventions,
See them lend love illustration
By gesture and grimace.
I watch them curiously, detect beneath the laughs
What stands for grief, a vague bewilderment
At things not turning right.

I sit at open windows in my shirt,
Observe, like some Jehovah of the west,
What passes by, that sanity be kept.

See, on gravel paths

See, on gravel paths under the harpstrung trees,
He steps so near the water that a swan's wing
Might play upon his lank locks with its wind,
The lake's voice and the rolling of mock waves
Make discord with the voice within his ribs
That thunders as heart thunders, slows as heart slows.
Is not his heart imprisoned by the summer
Snaring the whistles of the birds
And fastening in its cage the flowers' colour?
No, he's a stranger, outside the season's humour,
Moves, among men caught by the sun,

With heart unlocked upon the gigantic earth.
He alone is free, and, free, moans to the sky.
He, too, could touch the season's lips and smile,
Under the hanging branches hear the winds' harps.
But he is left. Summer to him
Is the ripening of apples,
The unbosoming of the sun,
And a delicate confusion in the blood.

So shall he step till summer loosens its hold
On the canvas sky, and all hot colours melt
Into the browns of autumn and the sharp whites of winter,
And so complain, in a vain voice, to the stars.

Even among his own kin is he lost,
Is love a shadow on the wall,
Among all living men is a sad ghost.
He is not man's nor woman's man,
Leper among a clean people
Walks with the hills for company,
And has the mad trees' talk by heart.

O lonely among many, the gods' man,
Knowing exceeding grief and the gods' sorrow
That, like a razor, skims, cuts, and turns,
Aches till the metal meets the marrow,
You, too, know the exceeding joy
And the triumphant crow of laughter.
Out of a bird's wing writing on a cloud
You capture more than man or woman guesses;
Rarer delight shoots in the blood
At the deft movements of the irises
Growing in public places than man knows;
There in the sunset and sunrise
Joy lifts its head, wonderful with surprise.
A rarer wonder is than man supposes.

See, on gravel paths under the harpstrung trees,

Feeling the summer wind, hearing the swans,
Leaning from windows over a length of lawns,
On level hills admiring the sea
Or the steeples of old towns
Stabbing the changing sky, he is alone,
Alone complains to the stars.
Who are his friends? The wind is his friend,
The glow-worm lights his darkness, and
The snail tells of coming rain.

The ploughman's gone

The ploughman's gone, the hansom driver,
Left in the records of living a not-to-be-broken picture,
In sun and rain working for good and gain,
Left only the voice in the old village choir
To remember, cast stricture on mechanics and man.
The windmills of the world still stand
With wooden arms revolving in the wind
Against the rusty sword and the old horse
Bony and spavined, rich with fleas.
But the horses are gone and the reins are green
As the hands that held them in my father's time.
The wireless snarls on the hearth.
Beneath a balcony the pianola plays
Black music to a Juliet in her stays
Who lights a fag-end at the flame of love.
No more toils over the fields
The rawboned horse to a man's voice
Telling it this, patting its black nose:
You shall go as the others have gone,
Lay your head on a hard bed of stone,
And have the raven for companion.
The ploughman's gone, the hansom driver,

Within his head revolved a little world
Masters over unmastered nature,
Soil's stock, street's stock, of the moon lit, ill lit, field and
                                                                town,
Lie cold, with their horses, for raven and kite.

Man toils now on an iron saddle, riding
In sun and rain over the dry shires,
Hearing the engines, and the wheat dying.
Sometimes at his ear the engine's voice
Revolves over and over again
The same tune as in my father's time:
You shall go as the others have gone,
Lay your head on a hard bed of stone,
And have the raven for companion.
It is the engine and not the raven.
Man who once drove is driven in sun and rain.
It is the engine for companion.
It is the engine under the unaltered sun.

Within his head revolved a little world

Within his head revolved a little world
Where wheels, confusing music, confused doubts,
Rolled down all images into the pits
Where half dead vanities were sleeping curled
Like cats, and lusts lay half hot in the cold.

Within his head the engines made their hell,
The veins at either temple whipped him mad,
And, mad, he called his curses upon God,
Spied moon-mad beasts carousing on the hill,
Mad birds in trees, and mad fish in a pool.
Across the sun was spread a crazy smile.
The moon leered down the valley like a fool.

Now did the softest sound of foot or voice
Echo a hundred times, the flight of birds
Drum harshly on the air, the lightning swords
Tear with a great sound through the skies,
And there was thunder in an opening rose.

All reason broke, and horror walked the roads.
A smile let loose a devil, a bell struck.
He could hear women breathing in the dark,
See women's faces under living snoods,
With serpents' mouths and scolecophidian voids
Where eyes should be, and nostrils full of toads.

Taxis and lilies to tinned music stept
A measure on the lawn where cupids blew
Water through every hole, a Sanger's show
Paraded up the aisles and in the crypt
Of churches made from abstract and concrete.
Pole-sitting girls descended for a meal,
Stopped non-stop dancing to let hot feet cool,
Or all-in wrestling for torn limbs to heal,
The moon leered down the valley like a fool.

Where, what's my God among this crazy rattling
Of knives on forks, he cried, of nerve on nerve,
Man's ribs on woman's, straight line on a curve,
And hand to buttock, man to engine, battling,
Bruising, where's God's my Shepherd, God is Love?
No loving shepherd in this upside life.

So crying, he was dragged into the sewer,
Voles at his armpits, down the sad canal
Where floated a dead dog who made him ill,
Plunged in black waters, under hail and fire,
Knee-deep in vomit. I saw him there,
And thus I saw him searching for his soul.

And swimming down the gutters he looks up

At cotton worlds revolving on a hip,
Riding on girders of the air, looks down
On garages and clinics in the town.

Where, what's my God among this taxi stepping,
This lily crawling round the local pubs?
It was November there were whizzbangs hopping,
But now there are the butt-ends of spent squibs.

So crying, he was pushed into the Jordan.
He, too, has known the agony in the Garden,
And felt a skewer enter at his side.
He, too, has seen the world as bottom rotten,
Kicked, with a clatter, ash-bins marked verboten,
And heard the teeth of weasels drawing blood.

And thus I saw him. He was poised like this,
One hand at head, the other at a loss,
Between the street-lamps and the ill-lit sky,
And thus, between the seasons, heard him cry:

Where, what's my God? I have been mad, am mad,
Have searched for shells and signs on the sea shore,
Stuck straw and seven stars upon my hair,
And leant on stiles and on the golden bar,
I have ridden on gutter dung and cloud.
Under a hideous sea where coral men
Feed in the armpits of drowned girls, I've swum
And sunk; waved flags to every fife and drum;
Said all the usual things over and again;
Lain with parched things; loved dogs and women;
I have desired the circle of the sun.
Tested by fire, double thumb to nose,
I've mocked the moving of the universe.
Where, what? There was commotion in the skies,
But no god rose. I have seen bad and worse,
Gibed the coitus of the stars. No god
Comes from my evil or my good. Mad, mad,

Feeling the pinpricks of the blood, I've said
The novel things. But it has been no good.

Crying such words, he left the crying crowds,
Unshackled the weights of words from tired limbs,
And took to feeding birds with broken crumbs
Of old divinities, split bits of names.
Very alone, he ploughed the only way.
And thus I saw him in a square of fields,
Knocking off turnip tops, with trees for friends,
And thus, some time later, I heard him say:

Out of the building of the day I've stept
To hermits' huts, and talked to ancient men.
Out of the noise into quiet I ran.
My God's a shepherd, God's the love I hoped.
The moon peers down the valley like a saint.
Taxis and lilies, noise and no noise,
Pair off, make harmonies, harmonious chord,
For he has found his soul in loneliness,
Now he is one with many, one with all,
Fire and Jordan and the sad canal.
Now he has heard and read the happy word.
Still, in his hut, he broods among his birds.
I see him in the crowds, not shut
From you or me or wind or rat
Or this or that.

The first ten years in school and park

The first ten years in school and park
Leapt like a ball from light to dark,
Bogies scared from landing and from corner,
Leapt on the bed, but now I've sterner
Stuff inside, dole for no work's

No turnip ghost now I'm no minor.
Dead are the days of thumbstained primer,
Outpourings of old soaks in censored books;
Brother spare a dime sounds louder
Than the academicians' thunder; sooner
Be fed with food than dreams. Still,
There was sense in Harrow on the Hill,
The playing fields of Eton, matchboard huts
Where youths learnt more than cigarettes and sluts,
Or on the coal tips near the engines
Where children played at Indians, scalps
Littered the raven Alps. There was meaning in this.
The next five years from morn to even
Hung between hell and heaven.
Plumbed devil's depths, reached angel's heights;
Dreams would have tempted saints at nights;
Night after night I climbed to bed,
The same thoughts in my head.
The last five years passed at a loss,
Fitting, all vainly, hopes dead as mown grass,
Fire and water of my young nonsense,
Height and depth, into the modern synthesis.
There were five years of trying
Mingling of living and dying.
So much of old and new, the old and new
Out of the war to make another,
Past and present, would not fit together,
And I, as you, was caught between
The field and the machine.
What was there to make of birds'
And factory's whistles but discords?
No music in the dynamo and harp.
Five years found no hope
Of harmony, no cure, till this year,
For bridging white and black,
The left and right sock, light and dark,
Pansy and piston, klaxon horn
And owl addressing moon.

Until you learn the keyboards, keys,
Struck down together, make harsh noise.
Follow this best of recipes.

Tune in to a tin organ at Toulouse,
Or in Appreciation Hour, run by the States,
Let pinches of tinned Mozart please,
Never forget, when hearing Bach on flutes,
Or after-dinner symphonies, that lots
Of people like that sound of noise,
Let cataracts of sound fall on your ears,
Listen in pain, till pain agrees.

That music understood, then there's another:
The music of turbine and lawn mower,
Hard, soft headed ecstasy,
Of plough and Ford along the earth,
Blackbird and Blue Bird, moth and Moth.

So much of old and new, the old and new
Out of the war to make another,
Past and present, will fit together
When the keys are no mysteries.
Twenty years; and now this year
Has found a cure.
New music, from new and loud, sounds on the air.

No man believes who, when a star falls shot

No man believes who, when a star falls shot,
Cries not aloud blind as a bat,
Cries not in terror when a bird is drawn
Into the quicksand feathers down,
Who does not make a wound in faith
When any light goes out, and life is death.

No man believes who cries not, god is not,
Who feels not coldness in the heat,
In the breasted summer longs not for spring,
No breasted girl, no man who, young
And green, sneers not at the old sky.
No man believes who does not wonder why.

Believe and be saved. No man believes
Who curses not what makes and saves,
No man upon this cyst of earth
Believes who does not lance his faith',
No man, no man, no man.

And this is true, no man can live
Who does not bury god in a deep grave
And then raise up the skeleton again,
No man who does not break and make,
Who in the bones finds not new faith,
Lends not flesh to ribs and neck,
Who does not break and make his final faith.

Children's Song

When I lie in my bed and the moon lies in hers,
And when neither of us can sleep
For the brotherly wind and the noise of the stars,
And the motherless cries of the sheep,
I think of a night when the owl is still
And the moon is hid and the stars are dim,
And that is the night that death will call,
And the night that I most fear him.
Let the owl hoot and the sheep complain;
Let the brotherly wind speak low;
Death shall not enter in west wind and rain,
Let the wind blow.

A woman wails her dead among the trees

(After the performance of Sophocles' Electra in a garden)

A woman wails her dead among the trees,
Under the green roof grieves the living;
The living sun laments the dying skies,
Lamenting falls. Pity Electra's loving

Of all Orestes' continent of pride
Dust in the little country of an urn,
Of Agamemnon and his kingly blood
That cries along her veins. No sun or moon

Shall lamp the raven darkness of her face,
And no Aegean wind cool her cracked heart;
There are no seacaves deeper than her eyes;
Day treads the trees and she the cavernous night.

Among the trees the language of the dead
Sounds, rich with life, out of a painted mask;
The queen is slain; Orestes' hands drip blood;
And women talk of horror to the dusk.

There can be few tears left: Electra wept
A country's tears and voiced a world's despair
At flesh that perishes and blood that's spilt
And love that goes down like a flower.

Pity the living who are lost, alone;
The dead in Hades have their host of friends,
The dead queen walketh with Mycenae's king
Through Hades' groves and the Eternal Lands.

Pity Electra loveless, she whose grief
Drowns and is drowned, who utters to the stars
Her syllables, and to the gods her love;
Pity the poor unpitied who are strange with tears.

Among the garden trees a pigeon calls,
And knows no woe that these sad players mouth
Of evil oracles and funeral ills;
A pigeon calls and women talk of death.

Praise to the architects

Praise to the architects;
Dramatic shadows in a tin box;
Nonstop; stoppress; vinegar from wisecracks;
Praise to the architects;
Radio's a building in the air;
The poster is today's text,
The message comes from negro mystics,
An old chatterbox, barenaveled at Nice,
Who steps on the gas;
Praise to the architects;
A pome's a buidling on a page;
Keatings is good for lice,
A pinch of Auden is the lion's feast;
Praise to the architects;
Empty, To Let, are signs on this new house;
To leave it empty's lion's or louse's choice;
Lion or louse? Take your own advice;
Praise to the architects.

We see rise the secret wind behind the brain

We see rise the secret wind behind the brain,
The sphinx of light sit on the eyes,
The code of stars translate in heaven.
A secret night descends between

The skull, the cells, the cabinned ears
Holding for ever the dead moon.

A shout went up to heaven like a rocket,
Woe from the rabble of the blind
Adorners of the city's forehead,
Gilders of streets, the rabble hand
Saluting the busy brotherhood
Of rod and wheel that wake the dead.

A city godhead, turbine moved, steel sculptured,
Glitters in the electric streets;
A city saviour, in the orchard
Of lamp-posts and high-volted fruits,
Speaks a steel gospel to the wretched
Wheel-winders and fixers of bolts.

We hear rise the secret wind behind the brain,
The secret voice cry in our ears,
The city gospel shout to heaven.
Over the electric godhead grows
One God, more mighty than the sun.
The cities have not robbed our eyes.

Love me, not as the dreamy nurses

Love me, not as the dreamy nurses
My falling lungs, nor as the cypress
In his age the lass's clay.
Love me and lift your mask.

Love me, not as the girls of heaven
Their airy lovers, nor the mermaiden
Her salt lovers in the sea.
Love me and lift your mask.

Love me, not as the ruffling pigeon
The tops of trees, nor as the legion
Of the gulls the lip of waves.
Love me and lift your mask.

Love me, as loves the mole his darkness
And the timid deer the tigress:
Hate the fear be your twin loves.
Love me and lift your mask.

Through these lashed rings

Through these lashed rings set deep inside their hollows
I eye the ring of earth, the airy circle,
My Maker's flesh that garments my clayfellows.
And through these trembling rings set in their valley
Whereon the hooded hair casts down its girdle,
A holy voice acquaints me with His glory.

Through these two rounded lips I pray to heaven,
Unending sea around my measured isle
The water spirit moves as it is bidden;
And, with not one fear-beggared syllable,
Praise God who springs and fills the tidal well;
Through this heart's pit I know His miracle.

And through these eyes God marks myself revolving,
And from these tongue-plucked senses draws his tune;
Inside this mouth I feel his message moving
Acquainting me with my divinity;
And through these ears he harks my fire burn
His awkward heart into some symmetry.

I see the boys of summer

I

I see the boys of summer in their ruin
Lay the gold tithings barren,
Setting no store by harvest, freeze the soils;
There in their heat the winter floods
Of frozen loves they fetch their girls,
And drown the cargoed apples in their tides.

These boys of light are curdlers in their folly,
Sour the boiling honey;
The jacks of frost they finger in the hives;
There in the sun the frigid threads
Of doubt and dark they feed their nerves;
The signal moon is zero in their voids.

I see the summer children in their mothers
Split up the brawned womb's weathers,
Divide the night and day with fairy thumbs;
There in the deep with quartered shades
Of sun and moon they paint their dams
As sunlight paints the shelling of their heads.

I see that from these boys shall men of nothing
Stature by seedy shifting,
Or lame the air with leaping from its heats;
There from their hearts the dogdayed pulse
Of love and light bursts in their throats.
O see the pulse of summer in the ice.

II

But seasons must be challenged or they totter
Into a chiming quarter
Where, punctual as death, we ring the stars;
There, in his night, the black-tongued bells

The sleepy man of winter pulls,
Nor blows back moon-and-midnight as she blows.

We are the dark deniers, let us summon
Death from a summer woman,
A muscling life from lovers in their cramp,
From the fair dead who flush the sea
The bright-eyed worm on Davy's lamp,
And from the planted womb the man of straw.

We summer boys in this four-winded spinning,
Green of the seaweeds' iron,
Hold up the noisy sea and drop her birds,
Pick the world's ball of wave and froth
To choke the deserts with her tides,
And comb the county gardens for a wreath.

In spring we cross our foreheads with the holly,
Heigh ho the blood and berry,
And nail the merry squires to the trees;
Here love's damp muscle dries and dies,
Here break a kiss in no love's quarry.
O see the poles of promise in the boys.

III

I see you boys of summer in your ruin.
Man in his maggot's barren.
And boys are full and foreign in the pouch.
I am the man your father was.
We are the sons of flint and pitch.
O see the poles are kissing as they cross.

Before I knocked

Before I knocked and flesh let enter,
With liquid hands tapped on the womb,
I who was shapeless as the water
That shaped the Jordan near my home
Was brother to Mnetha's daughter
And sister to the fathering worm.

I who was deaf to spring and summer,
Who knew not sun nor moon by name,
Felt thud beneath my flesh's armour,
As yet was in a molten form,
The leaden stars, the rainy hammer
Swung by my father from his dome.

I knew the message of the winter,
The darted hail, the childish snow,
And the wind was my sister suitor;
Wind in me leaped, the hellborn dew;
My veins flowed with the Eastern weather;
Ungotten I knew night and day.

As yet ungotten, I did suffer;
The rack of dreams my lily bones
Did twist into a living cipher,
And flesh was snipped to cross the lines
Of gallow crossed on the liver
And brambles in the wringing brains.

My throat knew thirst before the structure
Of skin and vein around the well
Where words and water make a mixture
Unfailing till the blood runs foul;
My heart knew love, my belly hunger;
I smelt the maggot in my stool.

And time cast forth my mortal creature
To drift or drown upon the seas
Acquainted with the salt adventure
Of tides that never touch the shores.
I who was rich was made the richer
By sipping at the vine of days.

I, born of flesh and ghost, was neither
A ghost nor man, but mortal ghost.
And I was struck down by death's feather.
I was mortal to the last
Long breath that carried to my father
The message of his dying christ.

You who bow down at cross and altar,
Remember me and pity Him
Who took my flesh and bone for armour
And doublecrossed my mother's womb.

My hero bares his nerves

My hero bares his nerves along my wrists
That rules from wrist to shoulder,
Unpacks the head that, like a sleepy ghost,
Leans on my mortal ruler,
The proud spine spurning turn and twist.

And these poor nerves so wired to the skull
Ache on the lovelorn paper
I hug to love with my unruly scrawl
That utters all love hunger
And tells the page the empty ill.

My hero bares my side and sees his heart
Tread, like a naked Venus,
The beach of flesh, and wind her bloodred plait;

Stripping my loin of promise,
He promises a secret heat.

He holds the wire from this box of nerves
Praising the mortal error
Of birth and death, the two sad knaves of thieves,
And the hunger's emperor;
He pulls the chain, the cistern moves.

Where once the waters of your face

Where once the waters of your face
Spun to my screws, your dry ghost blows,
The dead turns up its eye;
Where once the mermen through your ice
Pushed up their hair, the dry wind steers
Through salt and root and roe.

Where once your green knots sank their splice
Into the tided cord, there goes
The green unraveller,
His scissors oiled, his knife hung loose
To cut the channels at their source
And lay the wet fruits low.

Invisible, your clocking tides
Break on the lovebeds of the weeds;
The weed of love's left dry;
There round about your stones the shades
Of children go who, from their voids,
Cry to the dolphined sea.

Dry as a tomb, your coloured lids
Shall not be latched while magic glides
Sage on the earth and sky;

There shall be corals in your beds,
There shall be serpents in your tides,
Till all our sea-faiths die.

Our eunuch dreams

I

Our eunuch dreams, all seedless in the light,
Of light and love, the tempers of the heart,
Whack their boys' limbs,
And, winding-footed in their shawl and sheet,
Groom the dark brides, the widows of the night
Fold in their arms.

The shades of girls, all flavoured from their shrouds,
When sunlight goes are sundered from the worm,
The bones of men, the broken in their beds,
By midnight pulleys that unhouse the tomb.

II

In this our age the gunman and his moll,
Two one-dimensioned ghosts, love on a reel,
Strange to our solid eye,
And speak their midnight nothings as they swell;
When cameras shut they hurry to their hole
Down in the yard of day.

They dance between their arclamps and our skull,
Impose their shots, throwing the nights away;
We watch the show of shadows kiss or kill,
Flavoured of celluloid give love the lie.

III

Which is the world? Of our two sleepings, which
Shall fall awake when cures and their itch
Raise up this red-eyed earth?
Pack off the shapes of daylight and their starch,
The sunny gentlemen, the Welshing rich.
Or drive the night-geared forth.

The photograph is married to the eye,
Grafts on its bride one-sided skins of truth;
The dream has sucked the sleeper of his faith
That shrouded men might marrow as they fly.

IV

This is the world: the lying likeness of
Our strips of stuff that tatter as we move
Loving and being loth;
The dream that kicks the buried from their sack
And lets their trash be honoured as the quick.
This is the world. Have faith.

For we shall be a shouter like the cock,
Blowing the old dead back; our shots shall smack
The image from the plates;
And we shall be fit fellows for a life,
And who remain shall flower as they love,
Praise to our faring hearts.

Especially when the October wind

Especially when the October wind
With frosty fingers punishes my hair,
Caught by the crabbing sun I walk on fire
And cast a shadow crab upon the land,

By the sea's side, hearing the noise of birds,
Hearing the raven cough in winter sticks,
My busy heart who shudders as she talks
Sheds the syllabic blood and drains her words.

Shut, too, in a tower of words, I mark
On the horizon walking like the trees
The wordy shapes of women, and the rows
Of the star-gestured children in the park.
Some let me make you of the vowelled beeches,
Some of the oaken voices, from the roots
Of many a thorny shire tell you notes,
Some let me make you of the water's speeches.

Behind a pot of ferns the wagging clock
Tells me the hour's word, the neural meaning
Flies on the shafted disc, declaims the morning
And tells the windy weather in the cock.
Some let me make you of the meadow's signs;
The signal grass that tells me all I know
Breaks with the wormy winter through the eye.
Some let me tell you of the raven's sins.

Especially when the October wind
(Some let me make you of autumnal spells,
The spider-tongued, and the loud hill of Wales)
With fist of turnips punishes the land,
Some let me make you of the heartless words.
The heart is drained that, spelling in the scurry
Of chemic blood, warned of the coming fury.
By the sea's side hear the dark-vowelled birds.

When, like a running grave

When, like a running grave, time tracks you down,
Your calm and cuddled is a scythe of hairs,
Love in her gear is slowly through the house,
Up naked stairs, a turtle in a hearse,
Hauled to the dome,

Comes, like a scissors stalking, tailor age,
Deliver me who, timid in my tribe,
Of love am barer than Cadaver's trap
Robbed of the foxy tongue, his footed tape
Of the bone inch,

Deliver me, my masters, head and heart,
Heart of Cadaver's candle waxes thin,
When blood, spade-handed, and the logic time
Drive children up like bruises to the thumb,
From maid and head,

For, sunday faced, with dusters in my glove,
Chaste and the chaser, man with the cockshut eye,
I, that time's jacket or the coat of ice
May fail to fasten with a virgin o
In the straight grave,

Stride through Cadaver's country in my force,
My pickbrain masters morsing on the stone
Despair of blood, faith in the maiden's slime,
Halt among eunuchs, and the nitric stain
On fork and face.

Time is a foolish fancy, time and fool.
No, no, you lover skull, descending hammer
Descends, my masters, on the entered honour.
You hero skull, Cadaver in the hangar
Tells the stick 'fail'.

Joy is no knocking nation, sir and madam,
The cancer's fusion, or the summer feather
Lit on the cuddled tree, the cross of fever,
Nor city tar and subway bored to foster
Man through macadam.

I damp the waxlights in your tower dome.
Joy is the knock of dust, Cadaver's shoot
Of bud of Adam through his boxy shift,
Love's twilit nation and the skull of state,
Sir, is your doom.

Everything ends, the tower ending and,
(Have with the house of wind) the leaning scene,
Ball of the foot depending from the sun,
(Give, summer, over) the cemented skin,
The actions' end.

All, men my madmen, the unwholesome wind
With whistler's cough contages, time on track
Shapes in a cinder death; love for his trick,
Happy Cadaver's hunger as you take
The kissproof world.

In the beginning

In the beginning was the three-pointed star,
One smile of light across the empty face;
One bough of bone across the rooting air,
The substance forked that marrowed the first sun;
And, burning ciphers on the round of space,
Heaven and hell mixed as they spun.

In the beginning was the pale signature,
Three-syllabled and starry as the smile;

And after came the imprints on the water,
Stamp of the minted face upon the moon;
The blood that touched the crosstree and the grail
Touched the first cloud and left a sign.

In the beginning was the mounting fire
That set alight the weathers from a spark,
A three-eyed, red-eyed spark, blunt as a flower;
Life rose and spouted from the rolling seas,
Burst in the roots, pumped from the earth and rock
The secret oils that drive the grass.

In the beginning was the word, the word
That from the solid bases of the light
Abstracted all the letters of the void;
And from the cloudy bases of the breath
The word flowed up, translating to the heart
First characters of birth and death.

In the beginning was the secret brain.
The brain was celled and soldered in the thought
Before the pitch was forking to a sun;
Before the veins were shaking in their sieve,
Before shot and scattered to the winds of light
The ribbed original of love.

I fellowed sleep

I fellowed sleep who kissed me in the brain,
Let fall the tear of time; the sleeper's eye,
Shifting to light, turned on me like a moon.
So, 'planing-heeled, I flew along my man
And dropped on dreaming and the upward sky.

I fled the earth and, naked, climbed the weather,

Reaching a second ground far from the stars;
And there we wept, I and a ghostly other,
My mothers-eyed, upon the tops of trees;
I fled that ground as lightly as a feather.

'My fathers' globe knocks on its nave and sings.'
'This that we tread was, too, your fathers' land.'
'But this we tread bears the angelic gangs,
Sweet are their fathered faces in their wings.'
'These are but dreaming men. Breathe, and they fade.'

Faded my elbow ghost, the mothers-eyed,
As, blowing on the angels, I was lost
On that cloud coast to each grave-gabbing shade;
I blew the dreaming fellows to their bed
Where still they sleep unknowing of their ghost.

Then all the matter of the living air
Raised up a voice, and, climbing on the words,
I spelt my vision with a hand and hair,
How light the sleeping on this soily star,
How deep the waking in the worlded clouds.

There grows the hours' ladder to the sun,
Each rung a love or losing to the last,
The inches monkeyed by the blood of man.
An old, mad man still climbing in his ghost,
My fathers' ghost is climbing in the rain.

Incarnate devil

Incarnate devil in a talking snake,
The central plains of Asia in his garden,
In shaping-time the circle stung awake,
In shapes of sin forked out the bearded apple,
And God walked there who was a fiddling warden
And played down pardon from the heavens' hill.

When we were strangers to the guided seas,
A handmade moon half holy in a cloud,
The wisemen tell me that the garden gods
Twined good and evil on an eastern tree;
And when the moon rose windily it was
Black as the beast and paler than the cross.

We in our Eden knew the secret guardian
In sacred waters that no frost could harden,
And in the mighty mornings of the earth;
Hell in a horn of sulphur and the cloven myth,
All heaven in a midnight of the sun,
A serpent fiddled in the shaping-time.

Shall gods be said

Shall gods be said to thump the clouds
When clouds are cursed by thunder,
Be said to weep when weather howls?
Shall rainbows be their tunics' colour?

When it is rain where are the gods?
Shall it be said they sprinkle water
From garden cans, or free the floods?

Shall it be said that, venuswise,
An old god's dugs are pressed and pricked,
The wet night scolds me like a nurse?

It shall be said that gods are stone.
Shall a dropped stone drum on the ground,
Flung gravel chime? Let the stones speak
With tongues that talk all tongues.

Here in this spring

Here in this spring, stars float along the void;
Here in this ornamental winter
Down pelts the naked weather;
This summer buries a spring bird.
Symbols are selected from the years'
Slow rounding of four seasons' coasts,
In autumn teach three seasons' fires
And four birds' notes.

I should tell summer from the trees, the worms
Tell, if at all, the winter's storms
Or the funeral of the sun;
I should learn spring by the cuckooing,
And the slug should teach me destruction.

A worm tells summer better than the clock,
The slug's a living calendar of days;
What shall it tell me if a timeless insect
Says the world wears away?

Do you not father me

Do you not father me, nor the erected arm
For my tall tower's sake cast in her stone?
Do you not mother me, nor, as I am,
The lovers' house, lie suffering my stain?
Do you not sister me, nor the erected crime
For my tall turrets carry as your sin?
Do you not brother me, nor, as you climb,
Adore my windows for their summer scene?

Am I not father, too, and the ascending boy,
The boy of woman and the wanton starer

Marking the flesh and summer in the bay?
Am I not sister, too, who is my saviour?
Am I not all of you by the directed sea
Where bird and shell are babbling in my tower?
Am I not you who front the tidy shore,
Nor roof of sand, nor yet the towering tiler?
You are all these, said she who gave me the long suck,
All these, he said who sacked the children's town,
Up rose the Abraham-man, mad for my sake,
They said, who hacked and humoured, they were mine.
I am, the tower told, felled by a timeless stroke,
Who razed my wooden folly stands aghast,
For man-begetters in the dry-as-paste,
The ringed-sea ghost, rise grimly from the wrack.

Do you not father me on the destroying sand?
You are your sisters' sire, said seaweedy,
The salt sucked dam and darlings of the land
Who played the proper gentleman and lady.
Shall I still be love's house on the widdershin earth,
Woe to the windy masons at my shelter?
Love's to the windy masons at my shelter?
Love's house, they answer, and the tower death
Lie all unknowing of the grave sin-eater.

Hold hard, these ancient minutes

Hold hard, these ancient minutes in the cuckoo's month,
Under the lank, fourth folly on Glamorgan's hill,
As the green blooms ride upward, to the drive of time;
Time, in a folly's rider, like a county man
Over the vault of ridings with his hound at heel,
Drives forth my men, my children, from the hanging south.

Country, your sport is summer, and December's pools
By crane and water-tower by the seedy trees
Lie this fifth month unskated, and the birds have flown;
Hold hard, my country children in the world of tales,
The greenwood dying as the deer fall in their tracks,
This first and steepled season, to the summer's game.

And now the horns of England, in the sound of shape,
Summon your snowy horsemen, and the four-stringed hill,
Over the sea-gut loudening, sets a rock alive;
Hurdles and guns and railings, as the boulders heave,
Crack like a spring in a vice, bone breaking April,
Spill the lank folly's hunter and the hard-held hope.

Down fall four padding weathers on the scarlet lands,
Stalking my children's faces with a tail of blood,
Time, in a rider rising, from the harnessed valley;
Hold hard, my county darlings, for a hawk descends,
Golden Glamorgan straightens, to the falling birds.
Your sport is summer as the spring runs angrily.

Was there a time

Was there a time when dancers with their fiddles
In children's circuses could stay their troubles?
There was a time they could cry over books,
But time has set its maggot on their track.

Under the arc of the sky they are unsafe.
What's never known is safest in this life.
Under the skysigns they who have no arms
Have cleanest hands, and, as the heartless ghost
Alone's unhurt, so the blind man sees best.

Why east wind chills

Why east wind chills and south wind cools
Shall not be known till windwell dries
And west's no longer drowned
In winds that bring the fruit and rind
Of many a hundred falls;
Why silk is soft and the stone wounds
The child shall question all his days,
Why night-time rain and the breast's blood
Both quench his thirst he'll have a black reply.

When cometh Jack Frost? the children ask.
Shall they clasp a comet in their fists?
Not till, from high and low, their dust
Sprinkles in children's eyes a long-last sleep
And dusk is crowded with the children's ghosts,
Shall a white answer echo from the rooftops.

All things are known: the stars' advice
Calls some content to travel with the winds,
Though what the stars ask as they round
Time upon time the towers of the skies
Is heard but little till the stars go out.

I hear content, and 'Be content'
Ring like a handbell through the corridors,
And 'Know no answer,' and I know
No answer to the children's cry
Of echo's answer and the man of frost
And ghostly comets over the raised fists.

Ears in the turrets hear

Ears in the turrets hear
Hands grumble on the door,
Eyes in the gables see
The fingers at the locks.
Shall I unbolt or stay
Alone till the day I die
Unseen by stranger-eyes
In this white house?
Hands, hold you poison or grapes?
Beyond this island bound
By a thin sea of flesh
And a bone coast,
The land lies out of sound
And the hills out of mind.
No bird or flying fish
Disturbs this island's rest.

Ears in this island hear
The wind pass like a fire,
Eyes in this island see
Ships anchor off the bay.
Shall I run to the ships
With the wind in my hair,
Or stay till the day I die
And welcome no sailor?
Ships, hold you poison or grapes?

Hands grumble on the door,
Ships anchor off the bay,
Rain beats the sand and slates.
Shall I let in the stranger,
Shall I welcome the sailor,
Or stay till the day I die?

Hands of the stranger and holds of the ships,
Hold you poison or grapes?

Should lanterns shine

Should lanterns shine, the holy face,
Caught in an octagon of unaccustomed light,
Would wither up, and any boy of love
Look twice before he fell from grace.
The features in their private dark
Are formed of flesh, but let the false day come
And from her lips and faded pigments fall,
The mummy cloths expose an ancient breast.

I have been told to reason by the heart,
But heart, like head, leads helplessly;
I have been told to reason by the pulse,
And, when it quickens, alter the actions' pace
Till field and roof lie level and the same
So fast I move defying time, the quiet gentleman
Whose beard wags in Egyptian wind.

I have heard many years of telling,
And many years should see some change.

The ball I threw while playing in the park
Has not yet reached the ground.

I have longed to move away

I have longed to move away
From the hissing of the spent lie
And the old terrors' continual cry
Growing more terrible as the day
Goes over the hill into the deep sea;
I have longed to move away
From the repetition of salutes,
For there are ghosts in the air

And ghostly echoes on paper,
And the thunder of calls and notes.

I have longed to move away but am afraid;
Some life, yet unspent, might explode
Out of the old lie burning on the ground,
And, crackling into the air, leave me half-blind.
Neither by night's ancient fear,
The parting of hat from hair,
Pursed lips at the receiver,
Shall I fall to death's feather.
By these I would not care to die,
Half convention and half lie.

We lying by seasand

We lying by seasand, watching yellow
And the grave sea, mock who deride
Who follow the red rivers, hollow
Alcove of words out of cicada shade,
For in this yellow grave of sand and sea
A calling for colour calls with the wind
That's grave and gay as grave and sea
Sleeping on either hand.
The lunar silences, the silent tide
Lapping the still canals, the dry tide-master
Ribbed between desert and water storm,
Should cure our ills of the water
With a one-coloured calm:
The heavenly music over the sand
Sounds with the grains as they hurry
Hiding the golden mountains and mansions
Of the grave, gay, seaside land.
Bound by a sovereign strip, we lie,
Watch yellow, wish for wind to blow away

The strata of the shore and drown red rock;
But wishes breed not, neither
Can we fend off rock arrival,
Lie watching yellow until the golden weather
Breaks, O my heart's blood, like a heart and hill.

The spire cranes

The spire cranes. Its statue is an aviary.
From the stone nest it does not let the feathery
Carved birds blunt their striking throats on the salt gravel,
Pierce the spilt sky with diving wing in weed and heel
An inch in froth. Chimes cheat the prison spire, pelter
In time like outlaw rains on that priest, water,
Time for the swimmers' hands, music for silver lock
And mouth. Both note and plume plunge from the spire's
                                                    hook.
Those craning birds are choice for you, songs that jump
                                                    back
To the built voice, or fly with winter to the bells,
But do not travel down dumb wind like prodigals.

The hunchback in the park

The hunchback in the park
A solitary mister
Propped between trees and water
From the opening of the garden lock
That lets the trees and water enter
Until the Sunday sombre bell at dark

Eating bread from a newspaper
Drinking water from the chained cup
That the children filled with gravel
In the fountain basin where I sailed my ship
Slept at night in a dog kennel
But nobody chained him up.

Like the park birds he came early
Like the water he sat down
And Mister they called Hey mister
The truant boys from the town
Running when he had heard them clearly
On out of sound

Past lake and rockery
Laughing when he shook his paper
Hunchbacked in mockery
Through the loud zoo of the willow groves
Dodging the park keeper
With his stick that picked up leaves.

And the old dog sleeper
Alone between nurses and swans
While the boys among willows
Made the tigers jump out of their eyes
To roar on the rockery stones
And the groves were blue with sailors

Made all day until bell time
A woman figure without fault
Straight as a young elm
Straight and tall from his crooked bones
That she might stand in the night
After the locks and chains

All night in the unmade park
After the railings and shrubberies
The birds the grass the trees the lake

And the wild boys innocent as strawberries
Had followed the hunchback
To his kennel in the dark.

O make me a mask

O make me a mask and a wall to shut from your spies
Of the sharp, enamelled eyes and the spectacled claws
Rape and rebellion in the nurseries of my face,
Gag of a dumbstruck tree to block from bare enemies
The bayonet tongue in this undefended prayerpiece,
The present mouth, and the sweetly blown trumpet of lies,
Shaped in old armour and oak the countenance of a dunce
To shield the glistening brain and blunt the examiners,
And a tear-stained widower grief drooped from the lashes
To veil belladonna and let the dry eyes perceive
Others betray the lamenting lies of their losses
By the curve of the nude mouth or the laugh up the sleeve.

III

'Now I delight, I suppose, in
The countryman's return . . .'

The Countryman's Return

Embracing low-falutin
London (said the odd man in
A country pot, his hutch in
The fields, by a motherlike henrun)
With my fishtail hands and gently
Manuring popeye or
Swelling in flea-specked linen
The rankest of the city
I spent my unwasteable
Time among walking pintables
With sprung and padded shoulders,
Tomorrow's drunk club majors
Growing their wounds already,
The last war's professional
Unclaimed dead, girls from good homes
Studying the testicle
In communal crab flats
With the Sunflowers laid on,
Old paint-stained tumblers riding
On stools to a one man show down,
Gasketted and sirensuited
Bored and viciously waiting
Nightingales of the casualty stations
In the afternoon wasters
White feathering the living.

London's arches are falling
In, in Pedro's or Wendy's
With a silverfox farmer
Trying his hand at failing
Again, a collected poet
And some dismantled women,
Razor man and belly king,
I propped humanity's weight
Against the fruit machine,

Opened my breast and into
The spongebag let them all melt.
Zip once more for a traveller
With his goods under his eyes,
Another with hers under her belt,
The black man bleached to his tide
Mark, trumpet lipped and blackhead
Eyed, while the tears drag on the tail,
The weighing-scales, of my hand.
Then into blind streets I swam
Alone with my bouncing bag,
Too full to bow to the dim
Moon with a relation's face
Or lift my hat to unseen
Brothers dodging through the fog
The affectionate pickpocket
And childish, snivelling queen.

Beggars, robbers, inveiglers,
Voices from manholes and drains,
Maternal short time pieces,
Octopuses in doorways,
Dark inviters to keyholes
And evenings with great danes,
Bedsitting girls on the beat
With nothing for the metre,
Others whose single beds hold two
Only to make two ends meet,
All the hypnotised city's
Insidious procession
Hawking for money and pity
Among the hardly possessed.
And I in the wanting sway
Caught among never enough
Conjured me to resemble
A singing Walt from the mower
And jerrystone trim villas
Of the upper of the lower half,

Beardlessly wagging in Dean Street,
Blessing and counting the bustling
Twolegged handbagged sparrows,
Flogging into the porches
My cavernous, featherbed self.

Cut. Cut the crushed streets, leaving
A hole of errands and shades;
Plug the paper-blowing tubes;
Emasculate the seedy clocks;
Rub off the scrawl of prints on
Body and air and building;
Branch and leaf and birdless roofs;
Faces of melting visions,
Magdalene prostitution,
Glamour of the bloodily bowed,
Exaltation of the blind,
That sin-embracing dripper of fun
Sweep away like a cream cloud;
Bury all rubbish and love signs
Of my week in the dirtbox
In this anachronistic scene
Where sitting in clean linen
In a hutch in a cowpatched glen
Now I delight, I suppose, in
The countryman's return
And count by birds' eggs and leaves
The rusticating minutes,
The wasteful hushes among trees.
And O to cut the green field, leaving
One rich street with hunger in it.

Because the pleasure-bird whistles

Because the pleasure-bird whistles after the hot wires,
Shall the blind horse sing sweeter?
Convenient bird and beast lie lodged to suffer
The supper and knives of a mood.
In the sniffed and poured snow on the tip of the tongue of
                                        the year
That clouts the spittle like bubbles with broken rooms,
An enamoured man alone by the twigs of his eyes, two fires,
Camped in the drug-white shower of nerves and food,
Savours the lick of the times through a deadly wood of hair
In a wind that plucked a goose,
Nor ever, as the wild tongue breaks its tombs,
Rounds to look at the red, wagged root.
Because there stands, one story out of the bum city,
That frozen wife whose juices drift like a fixed sea
Secretly in statuary,
Shall I, struck on the hot and rocking street,
Not spin to stare at an old year
Toppling and burning in the muddle of towers and galleries
Like the mauled pictures of boys?
The salt person and blasted place
I furnish with the meat of a fable;
If the dead starve, their stomachs turn to tumble
An upright man in the antipodes
Or spray-based and rock-chested sea:
Over the past table I repeat this present grace.

After the funeral
(In memory of Ann Jones)

After the funeral, mule praises, brays,
Windshake of sailshaped ears, muffle-toed tap
Tap happily of one peg in the thick

Grave's foot, blinds down the lids, the teeth in black,
The spittled eyes, the salt ponds in the sleeves,
Morning smack of the spade that wakes up sleep,
Shakes a desolate boy who slits his throat
In the dark of the coffin and sheds dry leaves,
That breaks one bone to light with a judgment clout,
After the feast of tear-stuffed time and thistles
In a room with a stuffed fox and a stale fern,
I stand, for this memorial's sake, alone
In the snivelling hours with dead, humped Ann
Whose hooded, fountain heart once fell in puddles
Round the parched worlds of Wales and drowned each sun
(Though this for her is a monstrous image blindly
Magnified out of praise; her death was a still drop;
She would not have me sinking in the holy
Flood of her heart's fame; she would lie dumb and deep
And need no druid of her broken body).
But I, Ann's bard on a raised hearth, call all
The seas to service that her wood-tongued virtue
Babble like a bellbuoy over the hymning heads,
Bow down the walls of the ferned and foxy woods
That her love sing and swing through a brown chapel,
Bless her bent spirit with four, crossing birds.
Her flesh was meek as milk, but this skyward statue
With the wild breast and blessed and giant skull
Is carved from her in a room with a wet window
In a fiercely mourning house in a crooked year.
I know her scrubbed and sour humble hands
Lie with religion in their cramp, her threadbare
Whisper in a damp word, her wits drilled hollow,
Her fist of a face died clenched on a round pain;
And sculptured Ann is seventy years of stone.
These cloud-sopped, marble hands, this monumental
Argument of the hewn voice, gesture and psalm
Storm me forever over her grave until
The stuffed lung of the fox twitch and cry Love
And the strutting fern lay seeds on the black sill.

Once it was the colour of saying

Once it was the colour of saying
Soaked my table the uglier side of a hill
With a capsized field where a school sat still
And a black and white patch of girls grew playing;
The gentle seaslides of saying I must undo
That all the charmingly drowned arise to cockcrow and kill.
When I whistled with mitching boys through a reservoir
                                                    park
Where at night we stoned the cold and cuckoo
Lovers in the dirt of their leafy beds,
The shade of their trees was a word of many shades
And a lamp of lightning for the poor in the dark;
Now my saying shall be my undoing,
And every stone I wind off like a reel.

The tombstone told

The tombstone told when she died.
Her two surnames stopped me still.
A virgin married at rest.
She married in this pouring place,
That I struck one day by luck,
Before I heard in my mother's side
Or saw in the looking-glass shell
The rain through her cold heart speak
And the sun killed in her face.
More the thick stone cannot tell.

Before she lay on a stranger's bed
With a hand plunged through her hair,
Or that rainy tongue beat back
Through the devilish years and innocent deaths
To the room of a secret child,

Among men later I heard it said
She cried her white-dressed limbs were bare
And her red lips were kissed black,
She wept in her pain and made mouths,
Talked and tore though her eyes smiled.

I who saw in a hurried film
Death and this mad heroine
Meet once on a mortal wall
Heard her speak through the chipped beak
Of the stone bird guarding her:
I died before bedtime came
But my womb was bellowing
And I felt with my bare fall
A blazing red harsh head tear up
And the dear floods of his hair.

Poem in October

It was my thirtieth year to heaven
Woke to my hearing from harbour and neighbour
wood
And the mussel pooled and the heron
Priested shore
The morning beckon
With water praying and call of seagull and rook
And the knock of sailing boats on the net webbed wall
Myself to set foot
That second
In the still sleeping town and set forth.

My birthday began with the water-
Birds and the birds of the winged trees flying my name
Above the farms and the white horses
And I rose

      In rainy autumn
And walked abroad in a shower of all my days.
High tide and the heron dived when I took the road
         Over the border
            And the gates
Of the town closed as the town awoke.

    A springful of larks in a rolling
Cloud and the roadside bushes brimming with whistling
   Blackbirds and the sun of October
          Summery
       On the hill's shoulder,
Here were fond climates and sweet singers suddenly
Come in the morning where I wandered and listened
        To the rain wringing
          Wind blow cold
In the wood faraway under me.

    Pale rain over the dwindling harbour
And over the sea wet church the size of a snail
   With its horns through mist and the castle
         Brown as owls
        But all the gardens
Of spring and summer were blooming in the tall tales
Beyond the border and under the lark full cloud.
        There could I marvel
          My birthday
Away but the weather turned around.

    It turned away from the blithe country
And down the other air and the blue altered sky
   Streamed again a wonder of summer
         With apples
       Pears and red currants
And I saw in the turning so clearly a child's
Forgotten mornings when he walked with his mother
        Through the parables

Of sun light
And the legends of the green chapels

And the twice told fields of infancy
That his tears burned my cheeks and his heart moved in
mine.
These were the woods the river and sea
Where a boy
In the listening
Summertime of the dead whispered the truth of his joy
To the trees and the stones and the fish in the tide.
And the mystery
Sang alive
Still in the water and singingbirds.

And there could I marvel my birthday
Away but the weather turned around. And the true
Joy of the long dead child sang burning
In the sun.
It was my thirtieth
Year to heaven stood there then in the summer noon
Though the town below lay leaved with October blood.
O may my heart's truth
Still be sung
On this high hill in a year's turning.

A Winter's Tale

It is a winter's tale
That the snow blind twilight ferries over the lakes
And floating fields from the farm in the cup of the vales,
Gliding windless through the hand folded flakes,
The pale breath of cattle at the stealthy sail,

And the stars falling cold,

And the smell of hay in the snow, and the far owl
Warning among the folds, and the frozen hold
Flocked with the sheep white smoke of the farm house cowl
In the river wended vales where the tale was told.

Once when the world turned old
On a star of faith pure as the drifting bread,
As the food and flames of the snow, a man unrolled
The scrolls of fire that burned in his heart and head,
Torn and alone in a farm house in a fold

Of fields. And burning then
In his firelit island ringed by the winged snow
And the dung hills white as wool and the hen
Roosts sleeping chill till the flame of the cock crow
Combs through the mantled yards and the morning men

Stumble out with their spades,
The cattle stirring, the mousing cat stepping shy,
The puffed birds hopping and hunting, the milk maids
Gentle in their clogs over the fallen sky,
And all the woken farm at its white trades,

He knelt, he wept, he prayed,
By the spit and the black pot in the log bright light
And the cup and the cut bread in the dancing shade,
In the muffled house, in the quick of night,
At the point of love, forsaken and afraid.

He knelt on the cold stones,
He wept from the crest of grief, he prayed to the veiled sky
May his hunger go howling on bare white bones
Past the statues of the stables and the sky roofed sties
And the duck pond glass and the blinding byres alone

Into the home of prayers
And fires where he should prowl down the cloud
Of his snow blind love and rush in the white lairs.

His naked need struck him howling and bowed
Though no sound flowed down the hand folded air

But only the wind strung
Hunger of birds in the fields of the bread of water, tossed
In high corn and the harvest melting on their tongues.
And his nameless need bound him burning and lost
When cold as snow he should run the wended vales among

The rivers mouthed in night,
And drown in the drifts of his need, and lie curled caught
In the always desired centre of the white
Inhuman cradle and the bride bed forever sought
By the believer lost and the hurled outcast of light.

Deliver him, he cried,
By losing him all in love, and cast his need
Alone and naked in the engulfing bride,
Never to flourish in the fields of the white seed
Or flower under the time dying flesh astride.

Listen. The minstrels sing
In the departed villages. The nightingale,
Dust in the buried wood, flies on the grains of her wings
And spells on the winds of the dead his winter's tale.
The voice of the dust of water from the withered spring

Is telling. The wizened
Stream with bells and baying water bounds. The dew rings
On the gristed leaves and the long gone glistening
Parish of snow. The carved mouths in the rock are wind
                                    swept strings.
Time sings through the intricately dead snow drop. Listen.

It was a hand or sound
In the long ago land that glided the dark door wide
And there outside on the bread of the ground
A she bird rose and rayed like a burning bride.

A she bird dawned, and her breast with snow and scarlet
                                                    downed.

        Look. And the dancers move
On the departed, snow bushed green, wanton in moon light
As a dust of pigeons. Exulting, the grave hooved
Horses, centaur dead, turn and tread the drenched white
Paddocks in the farms of birds. The dead oak walks for love.

        The carved limbs in the rock
Leap, as to trumpets. Calligraphy of the old
Leaves is dancing. Lines of age on the stones weave in a
                                                    flock.
And the harp shaped voice of the water's dust plucks in a
                                                    fold
Of fields. For love, the long ago she bird rises. Look.

        And the wild wings were raised
Above her folded head, and the soft feathered voice
Was flying through the house as though the she bird praised
And all the elements of the slow fall rejoiced
That a man knelt alone in the cup of the vales,

        In the mantle and calm,
By the spit and the black pot in the log bright light.
And the sky of birds in the plumed voice charmed
Him up and he ran like a wind after the kindling flight
Past the blind barns and byres of the windless farm.

        In the poles of the year
When black birds died like priests in the cloaked hedge row
And over the cloth of counties the far hills rode near,
Under the one leaved trees ran a scarecrow of snow
And fast through the drifts of the thickets antlered like deer,

        Rags and prayers down the knee-
Deep hillocks and loud on the numbed lakes,
All night lost and long wading in the wake of the she-

Bird through the times and lands and tribes of the slow
　　　　　　　　　　　　　　　　　　　　　　flakes.
Listen and look where she sails the goose plucked sea,

　　　The sky, the bird, the bride,
The cloud, the need, the planted stars, the joy beyond
The fields of seed and the time dying flesh astride,
The heavens, the heaven, the grave, the burning font.
In the far ago land the door of his death glided wide,

　　　And the bird descended.
On a bread white hill over the cupped farm
And the lakes and floating fields and the river wended
Vales where he prayed to come to the last harm
And the home of prayers and fires, the tale ended.

　　　The dancing perishes
On the white, no longer growing green, and, minstrel dead,
The singing breaks in the snow shoed villages of wishes
That once cut the figures of birds on the deep bread
And over the glazed lakes skated the shapes of fishes

　　　Flying. The rite is shorn
Of nightingale and centaur dead horse. The springs wither
Back. Lines of age sleep on the stones till trumpeting dawn.
Exultation lies down. Time buries the spring weather
That belled and bounded with the fossil and the dew reborn.

　　　For the bird lay bedded
In a choir of wings, as though she slept or died,
And the wings glided wide and he was hymned and wedded,
And through the thighs of the engulfing bride,
The woman breasted and the heaven headed

　　　Bird, he was brought low,
Burning in the bride bed of love, in the whirl-
Pool at the wanting centre, in the folds

Of paradise, in the spun bud of the world.
And she rose with him flowering in her melting snow.

Once below a time

I

Once below a time,
When my pinned-around-the-spirit
Cut-to-measure flesh bit,
Suit for a serial sum
On the first of each hardship,
My paid-for slaved-for own too late
In love torn breeches and blistered jacket
On the snapping rims of the ashpit,
In grottoes I worked with birds,
Spiked with a mastiff collar,
Tasselled in cellar and snipping shop
Or decked on a cloud swallower,

Then swift from a bursting sea with bottlecork boats
And out-of-perspective sailors,
In common clay clothes disguised as scales,
As a he-god's paddling water skirts,
I astounded the sitting tailors,
I set back the clock faced tailors,

Then, bushily swanked in bear wig and tails,
Hopping hot leaved and feathered
From the kangaroo foot of the earth,
From the chill, silent centre
Trailing the frost bitten cloth,
Up through the lubber crust of Wales
I rocketed to astonish
The flashing needle rock of squatters,
The criers of Shabby and Shorten,
The famous stitch droppers.

II

My silly suit, hardly yet suffered for,
Around some coffin carrying
Birdman or told ghost I hung.
And the owl hood, the heel hider,
Claw fold and hole for the rotten
Head, deceived, I believed, my maker,

The cloud perched tailors' master with nerves for cotton.
On the old seas from stories, thrashing my wings,
Combing with antlers, Columbus on fire,
I was pierced by the idol tailor's eyes,
Glared through shark mask and navigating head,
Cold Nansen's beak on a boat full of gongs,

To the boy of common thread,
The bright pretender, the ridiculous sea dandy
With dry flesh and earth for adorning and bed.
It was sweet to drown in the readymade handy water
With my cherry capped dangler green as seaweed
Summoning a child's voice from a webfoot stone,
Never never oh never to regret the bugle I wore
On my cleaving arm as I blasted in a wave.

Now shown and mostly bare I would lie down,
Lie down, lie down and live
As quiet as a bone.

When I woke

When I woke, the town spoke.
Birds and clocks and cross bells
Dinned aside the coiling crowd,
The reptile profligates in a flame,

Spoilers and pokers of sleep,
The next-door sea dispelled
Frogs and satans and woman-luck,
While a man outside with a billhook,
Up to his head in his blood,
Cutting the morning off,
The warm-veined double of Time
And his scarving beard from a book,
Slashed down the last snake as though
It were a wand or subtle bough,
Its tongue peeled in the wrap of a leaf.

Every morning I make,
God in bed, good and bad,
After a water-face walk,
The death-stagged scatter-breath
Mammoth and sparrowfall
Everybody's earth.
Where birds ride like leaves and boats like ducks
I heard, this morning, waking,
Crossly out of the town noises
A voice in the erected air,
No prophet-progeny of mine,
Cry my sea town was breaking.
No Time, spoke the clocks, no God, rang the bells,
I drew the white sheet over the islands
And the coins on my eyelids sang like shells.

Holy Spring

O
Out of a bed of love
When that immortal hospital made one more move to
soothe
The cureless counted body,

And ruin and his causes
Over the barbed and shooting sea assumed an army
And swept into our wounds and houses,
I climb to greet the war in which I have no heart but only
That one dark I owe my light,
Call for confessor and wiser mirror but there is none
To glow after the god stoning night
And I am struck as lonely as a holy maker by the sun.

No
Praise that the spring time is all
Gabriel and radiant shrubbery as the morning grows joyful
Out of the woebegone pyre
And the multitude's sultry tear turns cool on the weeping
wall,
My arising prodigal
Sun the father his quiver full of the infants of pure fire,
But blessed be hail and upheaval
That uncalm still it is sure alone to stand and sing
Alone in the husk of man's home
And the mother and toppling house of the holy spring,
If only for a last time.

Fern Hill

Now as I was young and easy under the apple boughs
About the lilting house and happy as the grass was green,
The night above the dingle starry,
Time let me hail and climb
Golden in the heydays of his eyes,
And honoured among wagons I was prince of the apple
towns
And once below a time I lordly had the trees and leaves
Trail with daisies and barley
Down the rivers of the windfall light.

And as I was green and carefree, famous among the barns
About the happy yard and singing as the farm was home,
  In the sun that is young once only,
    Time let me play and be
   Golden in the mercy of his means,
And green and golden I was huntsman and herdsman, the
                calves
Sang to my horn, the foxes on the hills barked clear and
                 cold,
    And the sabbath rang slowly
   In the pebbles of the holy streams.

All the sun long it was running, it was lovely, the hay
Fields high as the house, the tunes from the chimneys, it was
                air
   And playing, lovely and watery
    And fire green as grass.
   And nightly under the simple stars
As I rode to sleep the owls were bearing the farm away,
All the moon long I heard, blessed among stables, the
               nightjars
   Flying with the ricks, and the horses
    Flashing into the dark.

And then to awake, and the farm, like a wanderer white
With the dew, come back, the cock on his shoulder: it was
                all
   Shining, it was Adam and maiden,
    The sky gathered again
   And the sun grew round that very day.
So it must have been after the birth of the simple light
In the first, spinning place, the spellbound horses walking
              warm
   Out of the whinnying green stable
    On to the fields of praise.

And honoured among foxes and pheasants by the gay house

Under the new made clouds and happy as the heart was
                                        long,
    In the sun born over and over,
       I ran my heedless ways,
   My wishes raced through the house high hay
And nothing I cared, at my sky blue trades, that time allows
In all his tuneful turning so few and such morning songs
    Before the children green and golden
      Follow him out of grace,

Nothing I cared, in the lamb white days, that time would
                                        take me
Up to the swallow thronged loft by the shadow of my hand,
    In the moon that is always rising,
      Nor that riding to sleep
   I should hear him fly with the high fields
And wake to the farm forever fled from the childless land.
Oh as I was young and easy in the mercy of his means,
    Time held me green and dying
    Though I sang in my chains like the sea.

IV

'A hill touches an angel . . .'

Laugharne

Off and on, up and down, high and dry, man and boy, I've
been living now for fifteen years, or centuries, in this
timeless, beautiful, barmy (both spellings) town, in this far,
forgetful, important place of herons, cormorants (known
here as billyduckers), castle, churchyard, gulls, ghosts,
geese, feuds, scares, scandals, cherry-trees, mysteries, jack-
daws in the chimneys, bats in the belfry, skeletons in the
cupboards, pubs, mud, cockles, flatfish, curlews, rain, and
human, often all too human, beings; and, though still very
much a foreigner, I am hardly ever stoned in the streets any
more, and can claim to be able to call several of the
inhabitants, and a few of the herons, by their Christian
names.

Now, some people live in Laugharne because they were
born in Laugharne and saw no good reason to move; others
migrated here, for a number of curious reasons, from places
as distant and improbable as Tonypandy or even England,
and have now been absorbed by the natives; some entered
the town in the dark and immediately disappeared, and can
sometimes be heard, on hushed black nights, making noises
in ruined houses, or perhaps it is the white owls breathing
close together, like ghosts in bed; others have almost
certainly come here to escape the international police, or
their wives; and there are those, too, who still do not know,
and will never know, why they are here at all: you can see
them, any day of the week, slowly, dopily, wandering up
and down the streets like Welsh opium-eaters, half asleep in
a heavy bewildered daze. And some, like myself, just came,
one day, for the day, and never left; got off the bus, and
forgot to get on again. Whatever the reason, if any, for our
being here, in this timeless, mild, beguiling island of a town
with its seven public-houses, one chapel in action, one
church, one factory, two billiard tables, one St Bernard
(without brandy), one policeman, three rivers, a visiting sea,
one Rolls-Royce selling fish and chips, one cannon (cast-

iron), one chancellor (flesh and blood), one port-reeve, one Danny Raye, and a multitude of mixed birds, here we just are, and there is nowhere like it anywhere at all.

But when you say, in a nearby village or town, that you come from this unique, this waylaying, old, lost Laugharne where some people start to retire before they start to work and where longish journeys, of a few hundred yards, are often undertaken only on bicycles, then, oh! the wary edging away, the whispers and whimpers, and nudges, the swift removal of portable objects!

'Let's get away while the going is good,' you hear.

'Laugharne's where they quarrel with boathooks.'

'All the women there's got web feet.'

'Mind out for the Evil Eye!'

'Never go there at the full moon!'

They are only envious. They envy Laugharne its minding of its own, strange, business; its sane disregard for haste; its generous acceptance of the follies of others, having so many, ripe and piping, of its own; its insular, featherbed air; its philosophy of 'It will all be the same in a hundred years' time.' They deplore its right to be, in their eyes, so wrong, and to enjoy it so much as well. And, through envy and indignation, they label and libel it a lengendary lazy little black-magical bedlam by the sea. And is it? Of *course not*, I hope.

In Country Sleep

I

Never and never, my girl riding far and near
In the land of the hearthstone tales, and spelled asleep,
Fear or believe that the wolf in a sheepwhite hood
Loping and bleating roughly and blithely shall leap,
                    My dear, my dear,

Out of a lair in the flocked leaves in the dew dipped year
To eat your heart in the house in the rosy wood.

Sleep, good, for ever, slow and deep, spelled rare and wise,
My girl ranging the night in the rose and shire
Of the hobnail tales: no gooseherd or swine will turn
Into a homestall king or hamlet of fire
      And prince of ice
To court the honeyed heart from your side before sunrise
In a spinney of ringed boys and ganders, spike and burn,

Nor the innocent lie in the rooting dingle wooed
And staved, and riven among plumes my rider weep.
From the broomed witch's spume you are shielded by fern
And flower of country sleep and the greenwood keep.
     Lie fast and soothed,
Safe be and smooth from the bellows of the rushy brood.
Never, my girl, until tolled to sleep by the stern

Bell believe or fear that the rustic shade or spell
Shall harrow and snow the blood while you ride wide and
         near,
For who unmanningly haunts the mountain ravened eaves
Or skulks in the dell moon but moonshine echoing clear
     From the starred well?
A hill touches an angel. Out of a saint's cell
The nightbird lauds through nunneries and domes of leaves

Her robin breasted tree, three Marys in the rays.
Sanctum sanctorum the animal eye of the wood
In the rain telling its beads, and the gravest ghost
The owl at its knelling. Fox and holt kneel before blood.
     Now the tales praise
The star rise at pasture and nightlong the fables graze
On the lord's table of the bowing grass. Fear most

For ever of all not the wolf in his baaing hood
Nor the tusked prince, in the ruttish farm, at the rind

And mire of love, but the Thief as meek as the dew.
The country is holy: O bide in that country kind,
              Know the green good,
Under the prayer wheeling moon in the rosy wood
Be shielded by chant and flower and gay may you

Lie in grace. Sleep spelled at rest in the lowly house
In the squirrel nimble grove, under linen and thatch
And star: held and blessed, though you scour the high four
Winds, from the dousing shade and the roarer at the latch,
              Cool in your vows.
Yet out of the beaked, web dark and the pouncing boughs
Be you sure the Thief will seek a way sly and sure

And sly as snow and meek as dew blown to the thorn,
This night and each vast night until the stern bell talks
In the tower and tolls to sleep over the stalls
Of the hearthstone tales my own, last love; and the soul
                                    walks
              The waters shorn.
This night and each night since the falling star you were
                                    born,
Ever and ever he finds a way, as the snow falls,

As the rain falls, hail on the fleece, as the vale mist rides
Through the haygold stalls, as the dew falls on the wind-
Milled dust of the apple tree and the pounded islands
Of the morning leaves, as the star falls, as the winged
              Apple seed glides,
And falls, and flowers in the yawning wound at our sides,
As the world falls, silent as the cyclone of silence.

II

Night and the reindeer on the clouds above the haycocks
And the wings of the great roc ribboned for the fair!
The leaping saga of prayer! And high, there, on the hare-
              Heeled winds the rooks

Cawing from their black bethels soaring, the holy books
Of birds! Among the cocks like fire the red fox

Burning! Night and the vein of birds in the winged, sloe
                                        wrist
Of the wood! Pastoral beat of blood through the laced
                                        leaves!
The stream from the priest black wristed spinney and
                                        sleeves
                  Of thistling frost
Of the nightingale's din and tale! The upgiven ghost
Of the dingle torn to singing and the surpliced

Hill of cypresses! The din and tale in the skimmed
Yard of the buttermilk rain on the pail! The sermon
Of blood! The bird loud vein! The saga from mermen
                  To seraphim
Leaping! The gospel rooks! All tell, this night, of him
Who comes as red as the fox and sly as the heeled wind.

Illumination of music! the lulled black backed
Gull, on the wave with sand in its eyes! And the foal moves
Through the shaken greensward lake, silent, on moonshod
                                        hooves,
                  In the winds' wakes.
Music of elements, that a miracle makes!
Earth, air, water, fire, singing into the white act,

The haygold haired, my love asleep, and the rift blue
Eyed, in the haloed house, in her rareness and hilly
High riding, held and blessed and true, and so stilly
                  Lying the sky
Might cross its planets, the bell weep, night gather her eyes,
The Thief fall on the dead like the willynilly dew,

Only for the turning of the earth in her holy
Heart! Slyly, slowly, hearing the wound in her side go
Round the sun, he comes to my love like the designed snow,

And truly he
Flows to the strand of flowers like the dew's ruly sea,
And surely he sails like the ship shape clouds. Oh he

Comes designed to my love to steal not her tide raking
Wound, nor her riding high, nor her eyes, nor kindled hair,
But her faith that each vast night and the saga of prayer
He comes to take
Her faith that this last night for his unsacred sake
He comes to leave her in the lawless sun awaking

Naked and forsaken to grieve he will not come.
Ever and ever by all your vows believe and fear
My dear this night he comes and night without end my dear
Since you were born:
And you shall wake, from country sleep, this dawn and each
first dawn,
Your faith as deathless as the outcry of the ruled sun.

Over Sir John's hill

Over Sir John's hill,
The hawk on fire hangs still;
In a hoisted cloud, at drop of dusk, he pulls to his claws
And gallows, up the rays of his eyes the small birds of the
bay
And the shrill child's play
Wars
Of the sparrows and such who swansing, dusk, in
wrangling hedges.
And blithely they squawk
To fiery tyburn over the wrestle of elms until
The flash the noosed hawk
Crashes, and slowly the fishing holy stalking heron
In the river Towy below bows his tilted headstone.

Flash, and the plumes crack,
And a black cap of jack-
Daws Sir John's just hill dons, and again the gulled birds
                                                    hare
To the hawk on fire, the halter height, over Towy's fins,
In a whack of wind.
There
Where the elegiac fisherbird stabs and paddles
In the pebbly dab filled
Shallow and sedge, and 'dilly dilly,' calls the loft hawk,
'Come and be killed,'
I open the leaves of the water at a passage
Of psalms and shadows among the pincered sandcrabs
                                                    prancing

And read, in a shell,
Death clear as a buoy's bell:
All praise of the hawk on fire in hawk-eyed dusk by sung,
When his viperish fuse hangs looped with flames under the
                                                    brand
Wing, and blest shall
Young
Green chickens of the bay and bushes cluck, 'dilly dilly,
Come let us die.'
We grieve as the blithe birds, never again, leave shingle and
                                                    elm,
The heron and I,
I young Aesop fabling to the near night by the dingle
Of eels, saint heron hymning in the shell-hung distant

Crystal harbour vale
Where the sea cobbles sail,
And wharves of water where the walls dance and the white
                                                    cranes stilt.
It is the heron and I, under judging Sir John's elmed
Hill, tell-tale the knelled
Guilt

Of the led-astray birds whom God, for their breast of
                                        whistles,
Have mercy on,
God in his whirlwind silence save, who marks the sparrows
                                        hail,
For their souls' song.
Now the heron grieves in the weeded verge. Through
                                        windows
Of dusk and water I see the tilting whispering

Heron, mirrored, go,
As the snapt feathers snow,
Fishing in the tear of the Towy. Only a hoot owl
Hollows, a grassblade blown in cupped hands, in the looted
                                        elms,
And no green cocks or hens
Shout
Now on Sir John's hill. The heron, ankling the scaly
Lowlands of the waves,
Makes all the music; and I who hear the tune of the slow,
Wear-willow river, grave,
Before the lunge of the night, the notes on this time-shaken
Stone for the sake of the souls of the slain birds sailing.

Poem on his Birthday

          In the mustardseed sun,
By full tilt river and switchback sea
          Where the cormorants scud,
In his house on stilts high among beaks
          And palavers of birds
This sandgrain day in the bent bay's grave
          He celebrates and spurns
His driftwood thirty-fifth wind turned age;
          Herons spire and spear.

Under and round him go
Flounders, gulls, on their cold, dying trails,
    Doing what they are told,
Curlews aloud in the congered waves
    Work at their ways to death,
And the rhymer in the long tongued room,
    Who tolls his birthday bell,
Toils towards the ambush of his wounds;
    Herons, steeple stemmed, bless.

In the thistledown fall,
He sings towards anguish; finches fly
    In the claw tracks of hawks
On a seizing sky; small fishes glide
    Through wynds and shells of drowned
Ship towns to pastures of otters. He
    In his slant, racking house
And the hewn coils of his trade perceives
    Herons walk in their shroud,

The livelong river's robe
Of minnows wreathing around their prayer;
    And far at sea he knows,
Who slaves to his crouched, eternal end
    Under a serpent cloud,
Dolphins dive in their turnturtle dust,
    The rippled seals streak down
To kill and their own tide daubing blood
    Slides good in the sleek mouth.

In a cavernous, swung
Wave's silence, wept white angelus knells.
    Thirty-five bells sing struck
On skull and scar where his loves lie wrecked,
    Steered by the falling stars.
And tomorrow weeps in a blind cage
    Terror will rage apart

Before chains break to a hammer flame
  And love unbolts the dark

  And freely he goes lost
In the unknown, famous light of great
  And fabulous, dear God.
Dark is a way and light is a place,
  Heaven that never was
Nor will be ever is always true,
  And, in that brambled void,
Plenty as blackberries in the woods
  The dead grow for His joy.

  There he might wander bare
With the spirits of the horseshoe bay
  Or the stars' seashore dead,
Marrow of eagles, the roots of whales
  And wishbones of wild geese,
With blessed, unborn God and His Ghost,
  And every soul His priest,
Gulled and chanter in young Heaven's fold
  Be at cloud quaking peace,

  But dark is a long way.
He, on the earth of the night, alone
  With all the living, prays,
Who knows the rocketing wind will blow
  The bones out of the hills,
And the scythed boulders bleed, and the last
  Rage shattered waters kick
Masts and fishes to the still quick stars,
  Faithlessly unto Him

  Who is the light of old
And air shaped Heaven where souls grow wild
  As horses in the foam:
Oh, let me midlife mourn by the shrined
  And druid herons' vows

The voyage to ruin I must run,
　　Dawn ships clouted aground,
Yet, though I cry with tumbledown tongue,
　　Count my blessings aloud:

　　Four elements and five
Senses, and man a spirit in love
　　Tangling through this spun slime
To his nimbus bell cool kingdom come
　　And the lost, moonshine domes,
And the sea that hides his secret selves
　　Deep in its black, base bones,
Lulling of spheres in the seashell flesh,
　　And this last blessing most,

　　That the closer I move
To death, one man through his sundered hulks,
　　The louder the sun blooms
And the tusked, ramshackling sea exults;
　　And every wave of the way
And gale I tackle, the whole world then
　　With more triumphant faith
Than ever was since the world was said
　　Spins its morning of praise,

　　I hear the bouncing hills
Grow larked and greener at berry brown
　　Fall and the dew larks sing
Taller this thunderclap spring, and how
　　More spanned with angels ride
The mansouled fiery islands! Oh,
　　Holier than their eyes,
And my shining men no more alone
　　As I sail out to die.

From **Under Milk Wood**
First Voice's Prologue

[*Silence*]

FIRST VOICE (*Very softly*)
     To begin at the beginning:
     It is spring, moonless night in the small town, starless and
     bible-black, the cobblestreets silent and the hunched,
     courters'-and-rabbits' wood limping invisible down to
     the sloeblack, slow, black, crowblack, fishingboat-
     bobbing sea. The houses are blind as moles (though moles
     see fine to-night in the snouting, velvet dingles) or blind as
     Captain Cat there in the muffled middle by the pump and
     the town clock, the shops in mourning, the Welfare Hall
     in widows' weeds. And all the people of the lulled and
     dumbfound town are sleeping now.
         Hush, the babies are sleeping, the farmers, the fishers,
     the tradesmen and pensioners, cobbler, school-teacher,
     postman and publican, the undertaker and the fancy
     woman, drunkard, dressmaker, preacher, policeman, the
     webfoot cocklewomen and the tidy wives. Young girls lie
     bedded soft or glide in their dreams, with rings and
     trousseaux, bridesmaided by glow-worms down the
     aisles of the organplaying wood. The boys are dreaming
     wicked or of the bucking ranches of the night and the
     jollyrodgered sea. And the anthracite statues of the horses
     sleep in the fields, and the cows in the byres, and the dogs
     in the wetnosed yards; and the cats nap in the slant
     corners or lope sly, streaking and needling, on the one
     cloud of the roofs.
         You can hear the dew falling, and the hushed town
     breathing. Only *your* eyes are unclosed to see the black
     and folded town fast, and slow, asleep. And you alone
     can hear the invisible starfall, the darkest-before-dawn
     minutely dewgrazed stir of the black, dab-filled sea where
     the *Arethusa*, the *Curlew* and the *Skylark*, *Zanzibar*,

Rhiannon, the *Rover*, the *Cormorant*, and the *Star of Wales* tilt and ride.

Listen. It is night moving in the streets, the processional salt slow musical wind in Coronation Street and Cockle Row, it is the grass growing on Llareggub Hill, dewfall, starfall, the sleep of birds in Milk Wood.

Listen. It is night in the chill, squat chapel, hymning in bonnet and brooch and bombazine black, butterfly choker and bootlace bow, coughing like nannygoats, sucking mintoes, fortywinking hallelujah; night in the four-ale, quiet as a domino; in Ocky Milkman's lofts like a mouse with gloves; in Dai Bread's bakery flying like black flour. It is to-night in Donkey Street, trotting silent, with seaweed on its hooves, along the cockled cobbles, past curtained fernpot, text and trinket, harmonium, holy dresser, watercolours done by hand, china dog and rosy tin teacaddy. It is night neddying among the snuggeries of babies.

Look. It is night, dumbly, royally winding through the Coronation cherry trees; going through the graveyard of Bethesda with winds gloved and folded, and dew doffed; tumbling by the Sailors Arms.

Time passes. Listen. Time passes.

Come closer now.

Only you can hear the houses sleeping in the streets in the slow deep salt and silent black, bandaged night. Only you can see, in the blinded bedrooms, the combs and petticoats over the chairs, the jugs and basins, the glasses of teeth, Thou Shalt Not on the wall, and the yellowing dickybird-watching pictures of the dead. Only you can hear and see, behind the eyes of the sleepers, the movements and countries and mazes and colours and dismays and rainbows and tunes and wishes and flight and fall and despairs the big seas of their dreams.

From where you are, you can hear their dreams.

Eli Jenkins's Verses to the Morning

SECOND VOICE
The Reverend Eli Jenkins, in Bethesda House, gropes out
of bed into his preacher's black, combs back his bard's
white hair, forgets to wash, pads barefoot downstairs,
opens the front door, stands in the doorway and, looking
out at the day and up at the eternal hill, and hearing the
sea break and the gab of birds, remembers his own verses
and tells them softly to empty Coronation Street that is
rising and raising its blinds.

REV. ELI JENKINS
Dear Gwalia! I know there are
Towns lovelier than ours,
And fairer hills and loftier far,
And groves more full of flowers,

And boskier woods more blithe with spring
And bright with birds' adorning,
And sweeter bards than I to sing
Their praise this beauteous morning.

By Cader Idris, tempest-torn,
Or Moel yr Wyddfa's glory,
Carnedd Llewelyn beauty born,
Plinlimmon old in story,

By mountains where King Arthur dreams,
By Penmaenmawr defiant,
Llareggub Hill a molehill seems,
A pygmy to a giant.

By Sawdde, Senny, Dovey, Dee,
Edw, Eden, Aled, all,
Taff and Towy broad and free,
Llyfnant with its waterfall,

Claerwen, Cleddau, Dulais, Daw,
Ely, Gwili, Ogwr, Nedd,
Small is our River Dewi, Lord,
A baby on a rushy bed.

By Carreg Cennen, King of time,
Our Heron Head is only
A bit of stone with seaweed spread
Where gulls come to be lonely.

A tiny dingle is Milk Wood
By Golden Grove 'neath Grongar,
But let me choose and oh! I should
Love all my life and longer

To stroll among our trees and stray
In Goosegog Lane, on Donkey Down,
And hear the Dewi sing all day,
And never, never leave the town.

SECOND VOICE
  The Reverend Jenkins closes the front door. His morning
  service is over.

                                              [*Slow bell notes*

The Children's Song

SECOND VOICE
  But with blue lazy eyes the fishermen gaze at that milk-
  mild whispering water with no ruck or ripple as though it
  blew great guns and serpents and typhooned the town.

FISHERMAN
  Too rough for fishing to-day.

SECOND VOICE
>And they thank God, and gob at a gull for luck, and
>moss-slow and silent make their way uphill, from the still
>still sea, towards the Sailors Arms as the children
>
>   [*School bell*

FIRST VOICE
>spank and scamper rough and singing out of school into
>the draggletail yard. And Captain Cat at his window says
>soft to himself the words of their song.

CAPTAIN CAT (*To the beat of the singing*)
>Johnnie Crack and Flossie Snail
>Kept their baby in a milking pail
>Flossie Snail and Johnnie Crack
>One would pull it out and one would put it back
>
>O it's my turn now said Flossie Snail
>To take the baby from the milking pail
>And it's my turn now said Johnny Crack
>To smack it on the head and put it back
>
>Johnnie Crack and Flossie Snail
>Kept their baby in a milking pail
>One would put it back and one would pull it out
>And all it had to drink was ale and stout
>For Johnnie Crack and Flossie Snail
>Always used to say that stout and ale
>Was *good* for a baby in a milking pail.   [*Long pause*

FIRST VOICE
>The music of the spheres is heard distinctly over Milk
>Wood. It is 'The Rustle of Spring'.

Polly Garter's Song

FIRST VOICE
The morning is all singing. The Reverend Eli Jenkins,
busy on his morning calls, stops outside the Welfare Hall
to hear Polly Garter as she scrubs the floors for the
Mothers' Union Dance to-night.

POLLY GARTER (*Singing*)
I loved a man whose name was Tom
He was strong as a bear and two yards long
I loved a man whose name was Dick
He was big as a barrel and three feet thick
And I loved a man whose name was Harry
Six feet tall and sweet as a cherry
But the one I loved best awake or asleep
Was little Willy Wee and he's six feet deep.

O Tom Dick and Harry were three fine men
And I'll never have such loving again
But little Willy Wee who took me on his knee
Little Willy Wee was the man for me.

Now men from every parish round
Run after me and roll me on the ground
But whenever I love another man back
Johnnie from the Hill or Sailing Jack
I always think as they do what they please
Of Tom Dick and Harry who were tall as trees
And most I think when I'm by their side
Of little Willy Wee who downed and died.

O Tom Dick and Harry were three fine men
And I'll never have such loving again
But little Willy Wee who took me on his knee
Little Willy Weazel was the man for me.

REV. ELI JENKINS
Praise the Lord! We are a musical nation.

SECOND VOICE
And the Reverend Jenkins hurries on through the town to visit the sick with jelly and poems.

Captain Cat and Rosie Probert

SECOND VOICE
One voice of all he remembers most dearly as his dream buckets down. Lazy early Rosie with the flaxen thatch, whom he shared with Tom-Fred the donkeyman and many another seaman, clearly and near to him speaks from the bedroom of her dust. In that gulf and haven, fleets by the dozen have anchored for the little heaven of the night; but she speaks to Captain napping Cat alone. Mrs Probert . . .

ROSIE PROBERT
from Duck Lane, Jack. Quack twice and ask for Rosie

SECOND VOICE
. . . is the one love of his sea-life that was sardined with women.

ROSIE PROBERT (*Softly*)
What seas did you see,
Tom Cat, Tom Cat,
In your sailoring days
Long long ago?
What sea beasts were
In the wavery green
When you were my master?

CAPTAIN CAT
  I'll tell you the truth.
  Seas barking like seals,
  Blue seas and green,
  Seas covered with eels
  And mermen and whales.

ROSIE PROBERT
  What seas did you sail
  Old whaler when
  On the blubbery waves
  Between Frisco and Wales
  You were my bosun?

CAPTAIN CAT
  As true as I'm here
  Dear you Tom Cat's tart
  You landlubber Rosie
  You cosy love
  My easy as easy
  My true sweetheart,
  Seas green as a bean
  Seas gliding with swans
  In the seal-barking moon.

ROSIE PROBERT
  What seas were rocking
  My little deck hand
  My favourite husband
  In your seaboots and hunger
  My duck my whaler
  My honey my daddy
  My pretty sugar sailor
  With my name on your belly
  When you were a boy
  Long long ago?

CAPTAIN CAT
  I'll tell you no lies.
  The only sea I saw
  Was the seesaw sea
  With you riding on it.
  Lie down, lie easy.
  Let me shipwreck in your thighs.

ROSIE PROBERT
  Knock twice, Jack,
  At the door of my grave
  And ask for Rosie.

CAPTAIN CAT
  Rosie Probert.

ROSIE PROBERT
  Remember her.
  She is forgetting.
  The earth which filled her mouth
  Is vanishing from her.
  Remember me.
  I have forgotten you.
  I am going into the darkness of the darkness for ever.
  I have forgotten that I was ever born.

CHILD
  Look,

FIRST VOICE
  says a child to her mother as they pass by the window of
  Schooner House,

CHILD
  Captain Cat is crying

Eli Jenkins's Sunset Poem

FIRST VOICE
> And at the doorway of Bethesda House, the Reverend
> Jenkins recites to Llareggub Hill his sunset poem.

REV. ELI JENKINS
> Every morning when I wake,
> Dear Lord, a little prayer I make,
> O please to keep Thy lovely eye
> On all poor creatures born to die.
>
> And every evening at sun-down
> I ask a blessing on the town,
> For whether we last the night or no
> I'm sure is always touch-and-go.
>
> We are not wholly bad or good
> Who live our lives under Milk Wood,
> And Thou, I know, wilt be the first
> To see our best side, not our worst.
>
> O let us see another day!
> Bless us all this night, I pray,
> And to the sun we all will bow
> And say, good-bye – but just for now!

Mr Waldo's Ballad

FIRST VOICE
> Llareggub Hill, writes the Reverend Jenkins in his poem-
> room,

REV. ELI JENKINS
> Llareggub Hill, that mystic tumulus, the memorial of

peoples that dwelt in the region of Llareggub before the
Celts left the Land of Summer and where the old wizards
made themselves a wife out of flowers.

SECOND VOICE
Mr Waldo, in his corner of the Sailors Arms, sings:

MR WALDO
In Pembroke City when I was young
I lived by the Castle Keep
Sixpence a week was my wages
For working for the chimbley-sweep.
Six cold pennies he gave me
Not a farthing more or less
And all the fare I could afford
Was parsnip gin and watercress.
I did not need a knife and fork
Or a bib up to my chin.
To dine on a dish of watercress
And a jug of parsnip gin.
Did you ever hear a growing boy
To live so cruel cheap
On grub that has no flesh and bones
And liquor that makes you weep?
Sweep sweep chimbley sweep,
I wept through Pembroke City
Poor and barefoot in the snow
Till a kind young woman took pity.
Poor little chimbley sweep she said
Black as the ace of spades
O nobody's swept my chimbley
Since my husband went his ways.
Come and sweep my chimbley
Come and sweep my chimbley
She sighed to me with a blush
Come and sweep my chimbley
Come and sweep my chimbley
Bring along your chimbley brush!

First Voice's Epilogue

FIRST VOICE

The thin night darkens. A breeze from the creased water sighs the streets close under Milk waking Wood. The Wood, whose every tree-foot's cloven in the black glad sight of the hunters of lovers, that is a God-built garden to Mary Ann Sailors who knows there is Heaven on earth and the chosen people of His kind fire in Llareggub's land, that is the fairday farmhands' wantoning ignorant chapel of bridesbeds, and, to the Reverend Eli Jenkins, a greenleaved sermon on the innocence of men, the suddenly wind-shaken wood springs awake for the second dark time this one Spring day.

Lament

When I was a windy boy and a bit
And the black spit of the chapel fold,
(Sighed the old ram rod, dying of women),
I tiptoed shy in the gooseberry wood,
The rude owl cried like a telltale tit,
I skipped in a blush as the big girls rolled
Ninepin down on the donkeys' common,
And on seesaw sunday nights I wooed
Whoever I would with my wicked eyes,
The whole of the moon I could love and leave
All the green leaved little weddings' wives
In the coal black bush and let them grieve.

When I was a gusty man and a half
And the black beast of the beetles' pews,
(Sighed the old ram rod, dying of bitches),
Not a boy and a bit in the wick-
Dipping moon and drunk as a new dropped calf,

I whistled all night in the twisted flues,
Midwives grew in the midnight ditches,
And the sizzling beds of the town cried, Quick! –
Whenever I dove in a breast high shoal,
Wherever I ramped in the clover quilts,
Whatsoever I did in the coal-
Black night, I left my quivering prints.

When I was a man you could call a man
And the black cross of the holy house,
(Sighed the old ram rod, dying of welcome),
Brandy and ripe in my bright, bass prime,
No springtailed tom in the red hot town
With every simmering woman his mouse
But a hillocky bull in the swelter
Of summer come in his great good time
To the sultry, biding herds, I said,
Oh, time enough when the blood creeps cold,
And I lie down but to sleep in bed,
For my sulking, skulking, coal black soul!

When I was a half of the man I was
And serve me right as the preachers warn,
(Sighed the old ram rod, dying of downfall),
No flailing calf or cat in a flame
Or hickory bull in milky grass
But a black sheep with a crumpled horn,
At last the soul from its foul mousehole
Slunk pouting out when the limp time came;
And I gave my soul a blind, slashed eye,
Gristle and rind, and a roarer's life,
And I shoved it into the coal black sky
To find a woman's soul for a wife.

Now I am a man no more no more
And a black reward for a roaring life,
(Sighed the old ram rod, dying of strangers),
Tidy and cursed in my dove cooed room

I lie down thin and hear the good bells jaw –
For, oh, my soul found a sunday wife
In the coal black sky and she bore angels!
Harpies around me out of her womb!
Chastity prays for me, piety sings,
Innocence sweetens my last black breath,
Modesty hides my thighs in her wings,
And all the deadly virtues plague my death!

In the White Giant's Thigh

Through throats where many rivers meet, the curlews cry,
Under the conceiving moon, on the high chalk hill,
And there this night I walk in the white giant's thigh
Where barren as boulders women lie longing still

To labour and love though they lay down long ago.

Through throats where many rivers meet, the women pray,
Pleading in the waded bay for the seed to flow
Though the names on their weed grown stones are rained
                                                away,

And alone in the night's eternal, curving act
They yearn with tongues of curlews for the unconceived
And immemorial sons of the cudgelling, hacked

Hill. Who once in gooseskin winter loved all ice leaved
In the courters' lanes, or twined in the ox roasting sun
In the wains tonned so high that the wisps of the hay
Clung to the pitching clouds, or gay with anyone
Young as they in the after milking moonlight lay

Under the lighted shapes of faith and their moonshade
Petticoats galed high, or shy with the rough riding boys,
Now clasp me to their grains in the gigantic glade,

Who once, green countries since, were a hedgerow of joys.

Time by, their dust was flesh the swineherd rooted sly,
Flared in the reek of the wiving sty with the rush
Light of his thighs, spreadeagle to the dunghill sky,
Or with their orchard man in the core of the sun's bush
Rough as cows' tongues and thrashed with brambles their
                                                    buttermilk
Manes, under his quenchless summer barbed gold to the
                                                    bone,

Or rippling soft in the spinney moon as the silk
And ducked and draked white lake that harps to a hail
                                                    stone.

Who once were a bloom of wayside brides in the hawed
                                                    house
And heard the lewd, wooed field flow to the coming frost,
The scurrying, furred small friars squeal, in the dowse
Of day, in the thistle aisles, till the white owl crossed

Their breast, the vaulting does roister, the horned bucks
                                                    climb
Quick in the wood at love, where a torch of foxes foams,
All birds and beasts of the linked night uproar and chime

And the mole snout blunt under his pilgrimage of domes,

Or, butter fat goosegirls, bounced in a gambo bed,
Their breasts full of honey, under their gander king
Trounced by his wings in the hissing shippen, long dead
And gone that barely dark where their clogs danced in the
                                                    spring,
And their firefly hairpins flew, and the ricks ran round –

(But nothing bore, no mouthing babe to the veined hives
Hugged, and barren and bare on Mother Goose's ground
They with the simple Jacks were a boulder of wives) –

Now curlew cry me down to kiss the mouths of their dust.

The dust of their kettles and clocks swings to and fro
Where the hay rides now or the bracken kitchens rust
As the arc of the billhooks that flashed the hedges low
And cut the birds' boughs that the minstrel sap ran red.
They from houses where the harvest kneels, hold me hard,
Who heard the tall bell sail down the Sundays of the dead
And the rain wring out its tongues on the faded yard,
Teach me the love that is evergreen after the fall leaved
Grave, after Beloved on the grass gulfed cross is scrubbed
Off by the sun and Daughters no longer grieved
Save by their long desirers in the fox cubbed
Streets or hungering in the crumbled wood: to these
Hale dead and deathless do the women of the hill
Love forever meridian through the courters' trees

And the daughters of darkness flame like Fawkes fires still.

V

'I'll put them all in a story by and by . . .'

The Orchards

He had dreamed that a hundred orchards on the road to the sea village had broken into flame; and all the windless afternoon tongues of fire shot through the blossom. The birds had flown up as a small red cloud grew suddenly from each branch; but as night came down with the rising of the moon and the swinging-in of the mile-away sea, a wind blew out the fires and the birds returned. He was an apple-farmer in a dream that ended as it began: with the flesh-and-ghost hand of a woman pointing to the trees. She twined the fair and dark tails of her hair together, smiled over the apple-fields to a sister figure who stood in a circular shadow by the walls of the vegetable garden; but the birds flew down on to her sister's shoulders, unafraid of the scarecrow face and the cross-wood nakedness under the rags. He gave the woman a kiss, and she kissed him back. Then the crows came down to her arms as she held him close; the beautiful scarecrow kissed him, pointing to the trees as the fires died.

Marlais awoke that summer morning, with his lips still wet from her kiss. This was a story more terrible than the stories of the reverend madmen in the Black Book of Llareggub, for the woman near the orchards, and her sister-stick by the wall, were his scarecrow lovers for ever and ever. What were the sea-village burning orchards and the clouds at the ends of the branches to his love for these bird-provoking women? All the trees of the world might blaze suddenly from the roots to the highest leaves, but he would not sprinkle water on the shortest fiery field. She was his lover, and her sister with birds on her shoulders held him closer than the women of LlanAsia.

Through the top-storey window he saw the pale blue, cloudless sky over the tangle of roofs and chimneys, and the promise of a lovely day in the rivers of the sun. There, in a chimney's shape, stood his bare, stone boy and the three blind gossips, blowing fire through their skulls, who

huddled for warmth in all weathers. What man on a roof
had turned his weathercock's head to stare at the red-and-
black girls over the town and, by his turning, made them
stone pillars? A wind from the world's end had frozen the
roof-walkers when the town was a handful of houses; now a
circle of coal table-hills, where the children played Indians,
cast its shadow on the black lots and the hundred streets;
and the stone-blind gossips cramped together by his bare
boy and the brick virgins under the towering crane-hills.

The sea ran to the left, a dozen valleys away, past the
range of volcanoes and the great stack forests and ten towns
in a hole. It met the Glamorgan shores where a half-
mountain fell westward out of the clump of villages in a
wild wood, and shook the base of Wales. But now, thought
Marlais, the sea is slow and cool, full of dolphins; it flows in
all directions from a green centre, lapping the land stones; it
makes the shells speak on the blazing half-mountain sand,
and the lines of time even shall not join the blue sea surface
and the bottomless bed.

He thought of the sea running; when the sun sank, a fire
went in under the liquid caverns. He remembered, while he
dressed, the hundred fires around the blossoms of the
apple-trees, and the uneasy salt rising of the wind that died
with the last pointing of the beautiful scarecrow's hand.
Water and fire, sea and apple-tree, two sisters and a crowd
of birds, blossomed, pointed, and flew down all that mid-
summer morning in a top-storey room in the house on a
slope over the black-housed town.

He sharpened his pencil and shut the sky out, shook back
his untidy hair, arranged the papers of a devilish story on his
desk, and broke the pencil-point with a too-hard scribble of
'sea' and 'fire' on a clean page. Fire would not set the ruled
lines alight, adventure, burning, through the heartless
characters, nor water close over the bogy heads and the
unwritten words. The story was dead from the devil up;
there was a white-hot tree with apples where a frozen tower
with owls should have rocked in a wind from Antarctica;
there were naked girls, with nipples like berries, on the sand

in the sun, where a cold and unholy woman should be wailing by the Kara Sea or the Sea of Azov. The morning was against him. He struggled with his words like a man with the sun, and the sun stood victoriously at high noon over the dead story.

Put a two-coloured ring of two women's hair round the blue world, white and coal-black against the summer-coloured boundaries of sky and grass, four-breasted stems at the poles of the summer sea-ends, eyes in the sea-shells, two fruit-trees out of a coal-hill: poor Marlais's morning, turned to evening, spins before you. Under the eyelids, where the inward night drove backwards, through the skull's base, into the wide, first world on the far-away eye, two love-trees smouldered like sisters. Have an orchard sprout in the night, an enchanted woman with a spine like a railing burn her hand in the leaves, man-on-fire a mile from a sea have a wind put out your heart: Marlais's death in life in the circular going down of the day that had taken no time blows again in the wind for you.

The world was the saddest in the turning world, and the stars in the north, where the shadow of a mock moon spun until a wind put out the shadow, were the ravaged south faces. Only the fork-tree breast of the woman's scarecrow could bear his head like an apple on the white wood where no worm would enter, and her barbed breast alone pierce the worm in the dream under her sweetheart's eyelid. The real round moon shone on the women of LlanAsia and the love-torn virgins of This street.

The word is too much with us. He raised his pencil so that its shadow fell, a tower of wood and lead, on the clean paper; he fingered the pencil tower, the half-moon of his thumb-nail rising and setting behind the leaden spire. The tower fell, down fell the city of words, the walls of a poem, the symmetrical letters. He marked the disintegration of the ciphers as the light failed, the sun drove down into a foreign morning, and the word of the sea rolled over the sun. 'Image, all image,' he cried to the fallen tower as the night came on. 'Whose harp is the sea? Whose burning candle is the sun?' An image of man, he rose to his feet and drew the curtains open. Peace, like a smile, lay over the roofs of the town. 'Image, all image,' cried Marlais, stepping through the window on to the level roofs.

The slates shone around him, in the smoke of the magnified stacks and through the vapours of the hill. Below him, in a world of words, men on their errands moved to no purpose but the escape of time. Brave in his desolation, he scrambled to the edge of the slates, there to stand perilously above the tiny traffic and the lights of the street signals. The toy of the town was at his feet. On went the marzipan cars, changing gear, applying brake, over the nursery carpets into a child's hands. But soon height had him and he swayed, feeling his legs grow weak beneath him and his skull swell like a bladder in the wind. It was the image of an infant city that threw his pulses into confusion. There was dust in his eyes; there were eyes in the grains of dust ascending from the street. Once on the leveller roofs, he touched his left breast. Death was the bright magnets of the streets; the wind pulled off the drag of death and the falling visions. Now he was stripped of fear, strong, night-muscled. Over the housetops he ran towards the moon. There the moon came, in a colder glory than before, attended by stars, drawing the tides of the sea. By a parapet he watched her, finding a word for each stage of her journey in the directed sky, calling her same-faced, wondering at her many masks. Death mask and dance mask over her mountainous features transformed the sky; she struggled behind a cloud, and came with a new smile over the wall of wind. Image, and all was image, from Marlais, ragged in the wind, to the appalling town, he on the roofs invisible to the street, the street beneath him blind to his walking word. His hand before him was five-fingered life.

A baby cried, but the cry grew fainter. It is all one, the loud voice and the still voice striking a common silence, the dowdy lady flattening her nose against the panes, and the well-mourned lady. The word is too much with us, and the dead word. Cloud, the last muslin's rhyme, shapes above tenements and bursts in cold rain on the suburban drives. Hail falls on cinder track and the angelled stone. It is all one, the rain and the macadam; it is all one, the hail and cinder, the flesh and the rough dust. High above the hum of the houses, far from the skyland and the frozen fence, he questioned each shadow; man among ghosts, and ghost in clover, he moved for the last answer.

The bare boy's voice through a stone mouth, no longer smoking at this hour, rose up unanswerably: 'Who walks, mad among us, on the roofs, by my cold, brick-red side and the weathercock-frozen women, walks over This street, under the image of the Welsh summer heavens walks all night loverless, has two sister lovers ten towns away. Past the great stack forests to the left and the sea his lovers burn for him endlessly by a hundred orchards.' The gossips' voices rose up unanswerably: 'Who walks by the stone virgins is our virgin Marlais, wind and fire, and the coward on the burning roofs.'

He stepped through the open window.

Red sap in the trees bubbled from the cauldron roots to the last spray of blossom, and the boughs, that night after the hollow walk, fell like candles from the trunks but could not die for the heat of the sulphurous head of the grass burned yellow by the dead sun. And flying there, he rounded, half mist, half man, all apple circles on the sea-village road in the high heat of noon as the dawn broke; and as the sun rose like a river over the hills so the sun sank behind a tree. The woman pointed to the hundred orchards and the black birds who flocked around her sister, but a wind put the trees out and he woke again. This was the intolerable, second waking out of a life too beautiful to break, but the dream was broken. Who had walked by the virgins near the orchards was a virgin, wind and fire, and a coward in the destroying coming of the morning. But after he had dressed and taken breakfast, he walked up This street to the hilltop and turned his face towards the invisible sea.

'Good morning, Marlais,' said an old man sitting with six greyhounds in the blackened grass.

'Good morning, Mr David Davies.'

'You are up very early,' said David Two Times.

'I am walking towards the sea.'

'The wine-coloured sea,' said Dai Twice.

Marlais strode over the hill to the greener left, and down behind the circle of the town to the rim of Whippet valley where the trees, for ever twisted between smoke and slag, tore at the sky and the black ground. The dead boughs prayed that the roots might shoulder up the soil, leaving a dozen channels empty for the leaves and the spirit of the cracking wood, a hole in the valley for the mole-handed sap, a long grave for the last spring's skeleton that once had leapt, when the blunt and forked hills were sharp and straight, through the once-green land. But Whippet's trees were the long dead of the stacked south of the country; who had vanished under the hacked land pointed, thumb-to-hill, these black leaf-nailed and warning fingers. Death in Wales had twisted the Welsh dead into those valley cripples.

The day was a passing of days. High noon, the story-killer and the fire bug (the legends of the Russian seas died as the trees awoke to their burning), passed in all the high noons since the fall of man from the sun and the first sun's pinnacling of the half-made heavens. And all the valley summers, the once monumental red and the now headstone-featured, all that midsummer afternoon were glistening in the seaward walk. Through the ancestral valley where his fathers, out of their wooden dust and full of sparrows, wagged at a hill, he walked steadily; on the brink of the hole that held LlanAsia as a grave holds a town, he was caught in the smoke of the forests and, like a ghost from the clear-cut quarters under the stack roots, climbed down on to the climbing streets.

'Where are you walking, Marlais?' said a one-legged man by a black flower-bed.

'Towards the sea, Mr William Williams.'

'The mermaid-crowded sea,' said Will Peg.

Marlais passed out of the tubercular valley on to a waste mountain, through a seedy wood to a shagged field; a crow, on a molehill, in Prince Price's skull cawed of the breadth of hell in the packed globe; the afternoon broke down, the stumped land heaving, and, like a tree or lightning, a wind, roots up, forked between smoke and slag as the dusk dropped; surrounded by echoes, the red-hot travellers of voices, and the devils from the horned acres, he shuddered on his enemies' territory as a new night came on in the nightmare of an evening. 'Let the trees collapse,' the dusty journeymen said, 'the boulders flake away and the gorse rot and vanish, earth and grass be swallowed down on to a hill's v balancing on the grave that proceeds to Eden. Winds on fire, through vault and coffin and fossil we'll blow a manfull of dust into the garden. Where the serpent sets the tree alight, and the apple falls like a spark out of its skin, a tree leaps up; a scarecrow shines on the cross-boughs, and, by one in the sun, the new trees arise, making an orchard round the crucifix.' By midnight two more valleys lay beneath him, dark with their two towns in the palms of the mined mountains; a valley, by one in the morning, held Aberbabel in its fist beneath him. He was a young man no longer but a legendary walker, a folk-man walking, with a cricket for a heart; he walked by Aberbabel's chapel, cut through the graveyard over the unstill headstones, spied a red-cheeked man in a nightshirt two foot above ground.

The valleys passed; out of the water-dipping hills, the moments of mountains, the eleventh valley came up like an hour. And coming out timelessly through the dwarf's eye of the telescope, through the ring of light like a circle's wedding on the last hill before the sea, the shape of the hundred orchards magnified with the immaculate diminshing of the moon. This was the spectacle that met the telescope, and the world Marlais saw in the morning following upon the first of the eleven untold adventures: to his both sides the unbroken walls, taller than the beanstalks that married a story on the roof of the world, of stone and earth and beetle and tree; a graveyard before him the ground came to a stop, shot down and down, was lost with the devil in bed, rose shakily to the sea-village road where the blossoms of the orchards hung over the wooden walls

and sister-roads ran off into the four white country points; a
rock line thus, straight to the hill-top, and the turning graph
scored with trees; dip down the county, deep as the history
of the final fire burning through the chamber one story over
Eden, the first green structure after the red downfall; down,
down, like a stone stuck with towns, like the river out of a
glass of places, fell his foot-holding hill. He was a folk-man
no longer but Marlais the poet walking, over the brink into
ruin, up the side of doom, over hell in bed to the red left, till
he reached the first of the fields where the unhatched apples
were soon to cry fire in a wind from a half-mountain falling
westward to the sea. A man-in-a-picture Marlais, by noon's
blow to the centre, stood by a circle of apple-trees and
counted the circles that travelled over the shady miles into a
clump of villages. He laid himself down in the grass, and
noon fell back bruised to the sun; and he slept till a handbell
rang over the fields. It was a windless afternoon in the
sisters' orchards, and the fair-headed sister was ringing the
bell for tea.

He had come very near to the end of the indescribable
journey. The fair girl, in a field sloping seaward three fields
and a stile from Marlais, laid out a white cloth on a flat
stone. Into one of a number of cups she poured milk and tea,
and cut the bread so thin she could see London through the
white pieces. She stared hard at the stile and the pruned,
transparent hedge, and as Marlais climbed over, ragged and
unshaven, his stripped breast burned by the sun, she rose
from the grass and smiled and poured tea for him. This was
the end to the untold adventures. They sat in the grass by the
stone table like lovers at a picnic, too loved to speak,
desireless familiars in the shade of the hedge corner. She had
shaken a handbell for her sister, and called a lover over
eleven valleys to her side. Her many lovers' cups were empty
on the flat stone.

And he who had dreamed that a hundred orchards had
broken into flame saw suddenly then in the windless
afternoon tongues of fire shoot through the blossom. The
trees all around them kindled and crackled in the sun, the

birds flew up as a small red cloud grew from each branch, the bark caught like gorse, the unborn, blazing apples whirled down devoured in a flash. The trees were fireworks and torches, smouldered out of the furnace of the fields into a burning arc, cast down their branded fruit like cinders on the charred roads and fields.

Who had dreamed a boy's dream of her flesh-and-ghost hand in the windless afternoon saw then, at the red height, when the wooden step-roots splintered at the orchard entrance and the armed towers came to grief, that she raised her hand heavily and pointed to the trees and birds. There was a flurry in the sky, of wing and fire and near-to-evening wind in the going below of the burned day. As the new night was built, she smiled as she had done in the short dream eleven valleys old; lame like Pisa, the night leaned on the west walls; no trumpet shall knock the Welsh walls down before the last crack of music; she pointed to her sister in a shadow by the disappearing garden, and the dark-headed figure with crows on her shoulders appeared at Marlais's side.

This was the end of a story more terrible than the stories of the quick and the undead in mountainous houses on Jarvis hills, and the unnatural valley that Idris waters is a children's territory to this eleventh valley in the seaward travel. A dream that was no dream skulked there; the real world's wind came up to kill the fires; a scarecrow pointed to the extinguished trees.

This he had dreamed before the blossom's burning and the putting-out, before the rising and the salt swinging-in, was a dream no longer near these orchards. He kissed the two secret sisters, and a scarecrow kissed him back. He heard the birds fly down on to his lovers' shoulders. He saw the fork-tree breast, the barbed eye, and the dry, twig hand.

The Enemies

It was morning in the green acres of the Jarvis valley, and
Mr Owen was picking the weeds from the edges of his
garden path. A great wind pulled at his beard, the vegetable
world roared under his feet. A rook had lost itself in the sky,
and was making a noise to its mate; but the mate never
came, and the rook flew into the west with a woe in its beak.
Mr Owen, who had stood up to ease his shoulders and look
at the sky, observed how dark the wings beat against the red
sun. In her draughty kitchen Mrs Owen grieved over the
soup. Once, in past days, the valley had housed the cattle
alone; the farm-boys came down from the hills to holla at
the cattle and to drive them to be milked; but no stranger set
foot in the valley. Mr Owen, walking lonely through the
country, had come upon it at the end of a late summer
evening when the cattle were lying down still, and the
stream that divided it was speaking over the pebbles. Here,
thought Mr Owen, I will build a small house with one
storey, in the middle of the valley, set around by a garden.
And, remembering clearly the way he had come along the
winding hills, he returned to his village and the questions of
Mrs Owen. So it came about that a house with one storey
was built in the green fields; a garden was dug and planted,
and a low fence put up around the garden to keep the cows
from the vegetables.

That was early in the year. Now summer and autumn had
gone over; the garden had blossomed and died; there was
frost at the weeds. Mr Owen bent down again, tidying the
path, while the wind blew back the heads of the nearby
grasses and made an oracle of each green mouth. Patiently
he strangled the weeds; up came the roots, making war in
the soil around them; insects were busy in the holes where
the weeds had sprouted, but, dying between his fingers, they
left no stain. He grew tired of their death, and tireder of the
fall of the weeds. Up came the roots, down went the cheap,
green heads.

Mrs Owen, peering into the depths of her crystal, had left

the soup to bubble on unaided. The ball grew dark, then lightened as a rainbow moved within it. Growing hot like a sun, and cooling again like an arctic star, it shone in the folds of her dress where she held it lovingly. The tea-leaves in her cup at breakfast had told of a dark stranger. What would the crystal tell her? Mrs Owen wondered.

Up came the roots, and a crooked worm, disturbed by the probing of the fingers, wriggled blind in the sun. Of a sudden the valley filled all its hollows with the wind, with the voice of the roots, with the breathing of the nether sky. Not only a mandrake screams; torn roots have their cries; each weed Mr Owen pulled out of the ground screamed like a baby. In the village behind the hill the wind would be raging, the clothes on the garden lines would be set to strange dances. And women with shapes in their wombs would feel a new knocking as they bent over the steamy tubs. Life would go on in the veins, in the bones, the binding flesh, that had their seasons and their weathers even as the valley binding the house about with the flesh of the green grass.

The ball, like an open grave, gave up its dead to Mrs Owen. She stared on the lips of women and the hairs of men that wound into a pattern on the face of the crystal world. But suddenly the patterns were swept away, and she could see nothing but the shapes of the Jarvis hills. A man with a black hat was walking down the paths into the invisible valley beneath. If he walked any nearer he would fall into her lap. 'There's a man with a black hat walking on the hills,' she called through the window. Mr Owen smiled and went on weeding.

It was at this time the Reverend Mr Davies lost his way; he had been losing it most of the morning, but now he had lost it altogether, and stood perturbed under a tree on the rim of the Jarvis hills. A great wind blew through the branches, and a great grey-green earth moved unsteadily beneath him. Wherever he looked the hills stormed up to the sky, and wherever he sought to hide from the wind he was frightened by the darkness. The farther he walked, the

stranger was the scenery around him; it rose to un-
dreamed-of heights, and then fell down again into a valley
no bigger than the palm of his hand. And the trees walked
like men. By a divine coincidence he reached the rim of the
hills just as the sun reached the centre of the sky. With the
wide world rocking from horizon to horizon, he stood
under a tree and looked down into the valley. In the fields
was a little house with a garden. The valley roared around
it, the wind leapt at it like a boxer, but the house stood still.
To Mr Davies it seemed as though the house had been
carried out of a village by a large bird and placed in the very
middle of the tumultuous universe.

But as he climbed over the craggy edges and down the side
of the hill, he lost his place in Mrs Owen's crystal. A cloud
displaced his black hat, and under the cloud walked a very
old phantom, a shape of air with stars all frozen in its beard,
and a half-moon for a smile. Mr Davies knew nothing of
this as the stones scratched his hands. He was old, he was
drunk with the wine of the morning, but the stuff that came
out of his cuts was a human blood.

Nor did Mr Owen, with his face near the soil and his
hands on the necks of the screaming weeds, know of the
transformation in the crystal. He had heard Mrs Owen
prophesy the coming of the black hat, and had smiled as he
always smiled at her faith in the powers of darkness. He had
looked up when she called, and, smiling, had returned to the
clearer call of the ground. 'Multiply, multiply,' he had said
to the worms disturbed in their channelling, and had cut the
brown worms in half so that the halves might breed and
spread their life over the garden and go out, contaminating,
into the fields and the bellies of the cattle.

Of this Mr Davies knew nothing. He saw a young man
with a beard bent industriously over the garden soil; he saw
that the house was a pretty picture, with the face of a pale
young woman pressed up against the window. And,
removing his black hat, he introduced himself as the rector
of a village some ten miles away.

'You are bleeding,' said Mr Owen.

Mr Davies's hands, indeed, were covered in blood.

When Mrs Owen had seen to the rector's cuts, she sat him down in the arm-chair near the window, and made him a strong cup of tea.

'I saw you on the hill,' she said, and he asked her how she had seen him, for the hills are high and a long way off.

'I have good eyes,' she answered.

He did not doubt her. Her eyes were the strangest he had seen.

'It is quiet here,' said Mr Davies.

'We have no clock,' she said, and laid the table for three.

'You are very kind.'

'We are kind to those that come to us.'

He wondered how many came to the lonely house in the valley, but did not question her for fear of what she would reply. He guessed she was an uncanny woman loving the dark because it was dark. He was too old to question the secrets of darkness, and now, with the black suit torn and wet and his thin hands bound with the bandages of the stranger woman, he felt older than ever. The winds of the morning might blow him down, and the sudden dropping of the dark be blind in his eyes. Rain might pass through him as it passes through the body of a ghost. A tired, white-haired old man, he sat under the window, almost invisible against the panes and the white cloth of the chair.

Soon the meal was ready, and Mr Owen came in unwashed from the garden.

'Shall I say grace?' asked Mr Davies when all three were seated around the table.

Mrs Owen nodded.

'O Lord God Almighty, bless this our meal,' said Mr Davies. Looking up as he continued his prayer, he saw that Mr and Mrs Owen had closed their eyes. 'We thank Thee for the bounties that Thou hast given us.' And he saw that the lips of Mr and Mrs Owen were moving softly. He could not hear what they said, but he knew that the prayers they spoke were not his prayers.

'Amen,' said all three together.

Mr Owen, proud in his eating, bent over the plate as he had bent over the complaining weeds. Outside the window was the brown body of the earth, the green skin of the grass, and the breasts of the Jarvis hills; there was a wind that chilled the animal earth, and a sun that had drunk up the dews on the fields; there was creation sweating out of the pores of the trees; and the grains of sand on far-away seashores would be multiplying as the sea rolled over them. He felt the coarse foods on his tongue; there was a meaning in the rind of the meat, and a purpose in the lifting of food to mouth. He saw, with a sudden satisfaction, that Mrs Owen's throat was bare.

She, too, was bent over her plate, but was letting the teeth of her fork nibble at the corners of it. She did not eat, for the old powers were upon her, and she dared not lift up her head for the greenness of her eyes. She knew by the sound which way the wind blew in the valley; she knew the stage of the sun by the curve of the shadows on the cloth. Oh, that she could take her crystal, and see within it the stretches of darkness covering up this winter light. But there was a darkness gathering in her mind, drawing in the light around her. There was a ghost on her left; with all her strength she drew in the intangible light that moved around him, and mixed it in her dark brains.

Mr Davies, like a man sucked by a bird, felt desolation in his veins, and, in a sweet delirium, told of his adventures on the hills, of how it had been cold and blowing, and how the hills went up and down. He had been lost, he said, and had found a dark retreat to shelter from the bullies in the wind; but the darkness had frightened him, and he walked again on the hills where the morning tossed him about like a ship on the sea. Wherever he went he was blown in the open or frightened in the narrow shades. There was nowhere, he said pityingly, for an old man to go. Loving his parish, he had loved the surrounding lands, but the hills had given under his feet or plunged him into the air. And, loving his God, he had loved the darkness where men of old had worshipped the dark invisible. But now the hill caves were full of shapes and voices that mocked him because he was old.

'He is frightened of the dark,' thought Mrs Owen, 'the lovely dark.' With a smile, Mr Owen thought: 'He is frightened of the worm in the earth, of the copulation in the tree, of the living grease in the soil.' They looked at the old man, and saw that he was more ghostly than ever. The window behind him cast a ragged circle of light round his head.

Suddenly Mr Davies knelt down to pray. He did not understand the cold in his heart nor the fear that bewildered him as he knelt, but, speaking his prayers for deliverance, he stared up at the shadowed eyes of Mrs Owen and at the smiling eyes of her husband. Kneeling on the carpet at the head of the table, he stared in bewilderment at the dark mind and the gross dark body. He stared and he prayed, like an old god beset by his enemies.

A Prospect of the Sea

It was high summer, and the boy was lying in the corn. He was happy because he had no work to do and the weather was hot. He heard the corn sway from side to side above him, and the noise of the birds who whistled from the branches of the trees that hid the house. Lying flat on his back, he stared up into the unbrokenly blue sky falling over the edge of the corn. The wind, after the warm rain before noon, smelt of rabbits and cattle. He stretched himself like a cat, and put his arms behind his head. Now he was riding on the sea, swimming through the golden corn waves, gliding along the heavens like a bird; in seven-league boots he was springing over the fields; he was building a nest in the sixth of the seven trees that waved their hands from a bright, green hill. Now he was a boy with tousled hair, rising lazily to his feet, wandering out of the corn to the strip of river by the hillside. He put his fingers in the water, making a mock sea-wave to roll the stones over and shake the weeds; his fingers stood up like ten tower pillars in the magnifying water, and a fish with a wise head and a lashing tail swam in and out of the tower gates. He made up a story as the fish swam through the gates into the pebbles and the moving bed. There was a drowned princess from a Christmas book, with her shoulders broken and her two red pigtails stretched like the strings of a fiddle over her broken throat; she was caught in a fisherman's net, and the fish plucked her hair. He forgot how the story ended, if ever there were an end to a story that had no beginning. Did the princess live again, rising like a mermaid from the net, or did a prince from another story tauten the tails of her hair and bend her shoulder-bone into a harp and pluck the dead, black tunes for ever in the courts of the royal country? The boy sent a stone skidding over the green water. He saw a rabbit scuttle, and threw a stone at its tail. A fish leaped at the gnats, and a lark darted out of the green earth. This was the best summer since the first seasons of the world. He did not believe in God, but God had made this summer full of blue winds and heat and pigeons in the house wood. There were no chimneys on the hills with no name in the distance, only the trees which stood like women and men enjoying the sun; there were no cranes or coal-tips, only the nameless distance and the hill with seven trees. He could think of no words to say how wonderful the summer was, or the noise of the wood-pigeons, or the lazy corn blowing in the half wind from the sea at the river's end. There were no words for the sky and the sun and the summer country: the birds were nice, and the corn was nice.

He crossed the nice field and climbed the hill. Under the innocent green of the trees, as blackbirds flew out towards the sun, the story of the princess died. That afternoon there was no drowning sea to pull her pigtails; the sea had flowed and vanished, leaving a hill, a cornfield, and a hidden house; tall as the first short tree, she clambered down from the seventh, and stood in front of him in a torn cotton frock. Her bare brown legs were scratched all over, there were berry stains round her mouth, her nails were black and broken, and her toes poked through her rubber shoes. She stood on a hill no bigger than a house, but the field below and the shining strip of river were as little as though the hill were a mountain rising over a single blade and a drop of water; the trees round the farmhouse were firesticks; and the Jarvis peaks, and Cader peak beyond them to the edge of England, were molehills and stones' shadows in the still, single yard of the distance. From the first shade, the boy stared down at the river disappearing, the corn blowing back into the soil, the hundred house trees dwindling to a stalk, and the four corners of the yellow field meeting in a square that he could cover with his hand. He saw the many-coloured county shrink like a coat in the wash. Then a new wind sprang from the pennyworth of water at the river-drop's end, blowing the hill to its full size, and the corn stood up as before, and the one stalk that hid the house was split into a hundred trees. It happened in a half second.

Blackbirds again flew out from the topmost boughs in a cloud like a cone; there was no end to the black, triangular flight of birds towards the sun; from hill to sun the winged bridge mounted silently; and then again a wind blew up, and this time from the vast and proper sea, and snapped the bridge's back. Like partridges the common birds fell down in a shower.

All of it happened in half a second. The girl in the torn cotton frock sat down on the grass and crossed her legs; a real wind from nowhere lifted her frock, and up to her waist she was brown as an acorn. The boy, still standing timidly in the first shade, saw the broken, holiday princess die for the second time, and a country girl take her place on the live hill. Who had been frightened of a few birds flying out of the trees, and a sudden daze of the sun that made river and field and distance look so little under the hill? Who had told him the girl was as tall as a tree? She was no taller or stranger than the flowery girls on Sundays who picnicked in Whippet valley.

'What were you doing up the tree?' he asked her, ashamed of his silence in front of her smiling, and suddenly shy as she moved so that the grass beneath her rose bent and green between her brown legs. 'Were you after nests?' he said, and sat down beside her. But on the bent grass in the seventh shade, his first terror of her sprang up again like a sun returning from the sea that sank it, and burned his eyes to the skull and raised his hair. The stain on her lips was blood, not berries; and her nails were not broken but sharpened sideways, ten black scissor-blades ready to snip off his tongue. If he cried aloud to his uncle in the hidden house, she would make new animals, beckon Carmarthen tigers out of the mile-away wood to jump around him and bite his hands; she would make new, noisy birds in the air to whistle and chatter away his cries. He sat very still by her left side, and heard the heart in her breast drown every summer sound; every leaf of the tree that shaded them grew to man-size then, the ribs of the bark were channels and rivers wide as a great ship; and the moss on the tree, and the sharp grass ring round the base, were all the velvet coverings of green county's meadows blown hedge to hedge. Now on the world-sized hill, with the trees like heavens holding up the weathers, in the magnified summer weather she leaned towards him so that he could not see the cornfield nor his uncle's house for her thick, red hair; and sky and far ridge were points of light in the pupils of her eyes.

This is death, said the boy to himself, consumption and whooping-cough and the stones inside you . . . and the way your face stays if you make too many faces in the looking-glass. Her mouth was an inch from his. Her long forefingers touched his eyelids. This is a story, he said to himself, about a boy on a holiday kissed by a broom-rider; she flew from a tree on to a hill that changes its size like a frog that loses its temper; she stroked his eyes and put her chest against him; and when she had loved him until he died she carried him off inside her to a den in a wood. But the story, like all stories, was killed as she kissed him; now he was a boy in a girl's arms, and the hill stood above a true river, and the peaks and their trees towards England were as Jarvis had known them when he walked there with his lovers and horses for half a century, a century ago.

Who had been frightened of a wind out of the light swelling the small country? The piece of a wind in the sun was like the wind in an empty house; it made the corners mountains and crowded the attics with shadows who broke through the roof; through the country corridors it raced in a hundred voices, each voice larger than the last, until the last voice tumbled down and the house was full of whispers.

'Where do you come from?' she whispered in his ear. She took her arms away but still sat close, one knee between his legs, one hand on his hands. Who had been frightened of a sunburned girl no taller or stranger than the pale girls at home who had babies before they were married?

'I come from Amman valley,' said the boy.

'I have a sister in Egypt,' she said, 'who lives in a pyramid . . .' She drew him closer.

'They're calling me in for tea,' he said.

She lifted her frock to her waist.

If she loves me until I die, said the boy to himself under the seventh tree on the hill that was never the same for three minutes, she will carry me away inside her, run with me rattling inside her to a den in a wood, to a hole in a tree where my uncle will never find me. This is the story of a boy being stolen. She has put a knife in my belly and turned my stomach round.

She whispered in his ear: 'I'll have a baby on every hill; what's your name, Amman?'

The afternoon was dying; lazily, namelessly drifting westward through the insects in the shade; over hill and tree and river and corn and grass to the evening shaping in the sea; blowing away; being blown from Wales in a wind, in the slow, blue grains, like a wind full of dreams and medicines; down the tide of the sun on to the grey and chanting store where the birds from Noah's ark glide by with bushes in their mouths, and tomorrow and tomorrow tower over the cracked sand-castles.

So she stroked her clothes into place and patted her hair as the day began to die, she rolled over on to her left side, careless of the low sun and the darkening miles. The boy awoke cautiously into a more curious dream, a summer vision broader than the one black cloud poised in the unbroken centre on a tower shaft of light; he came out of love through a wind full of turning knives and a cave full of flesh-white birds on to a new summit, standing like a stone that faces the stars blowing and stands no ceremony from the sea wind, a hard boy angry on a mound in the middle of a country evening; he put out his chest and said hard words to the world. Out of love he came marching, head on high, through a cave between two doors to a vantage hall room with an iron view over the earth. He walked to the last rail before pitch space; though the earth bowled round quickly, he saw every plough crease and beast's print, man track and water drop, comb, crest, and plume mark, dust and death groove and signature and time-cast shade, from icefield to icefield, sea rims to sea centres, all over the apple-shaped ball under the metal rails beyond the living doors. He saw through the black thumbprint of a man's city to the fossil thumb of a once-lively man of meadows; through the grass and clover fossil of the country print to the whole hand of a forgotten city drowned under Europe; through the hand-print to the arm of an empire broken like Venus; through the arm to the breast, from history to the thigh, through the thigh in the dark to the first and West print between the dark and the green Eden; and the garden was undrowned, to this next minute and for ever, under Asia in the earth that rolled on to its music in the beginning evening. When God was sleeping, he had climbed a ladder, and the room three jumps above the final rung was roofed and floored with the live pages of the book of days; the pages were gardens, the built words were trees, and Eden grew above him into Eden, and Eden grew down to Eden through the lower earth, an endless corridor of boughs and birds and leaves. He stood on a slope no wider than the loving room of the world, and the two poles kissed behind his shoulders; the boy stumbled forward like Atlas, loped over the iron view through the cave of knives and the capsized overgrowths of time to the hill in the field that had been a short mark under the platform in the clouds over the multiplying gardens.

'Wake up,' she said into his ear; the iron characters were broken in her smile, and Eden shrank into the seventh shade. She told him to look in her eyes. He had thought that her eyes were brown or green, but they were sea-blue with black lashes, and her thick hair was black. She rumpled his hair, and put his hand deep in her breast so that he knew the nipple of her heart was red. He looked in her eyes, but they made a round glass of the sun, and as he moved sharply away he saw through the transparent trees; she could make a long crystal of each tree, and turn the house wood into gauze. She told him her name, but he had forgotten it as she spoke; she told him her age, and it was a new number. 'Look in my eyes,' she said. It was only an hour to the proper night, the stars were coming out and the moon was ready. She took his hand and led him racing between trees over the ridge of the dewy hill, over the flowering nettles and the shut grass-flowers, over the silence into sunlight and the noise of a sea breaking on sand and stone.

The hill in a screen of trees: between the incountry fields and the incoming sea, night on the wood and the stained beach yellow in the sun, the vanishing corn through the ten dry miles of farmland and the golden wastes where the split sand lapped over rocks, it stood between time over a secret root. The hill in two searchlights: the back moon shone on seven trees, and the sun of a strange day moved above water in the spluttering foreground. The hill between an owl and a seagull: the boy heard two birds' voices as brown wings climbed through the branches and the white wings before him fluttered on the sea waves. 'Tu wit tu woo, do not adventure any more.' Now the gulls that swam in the sky told him to race on along the warm sand until the water hugged him to its waves and the spindrift tore around him like a wind and a chain. The girl had her hand in his, and she rubbed her cheek on his shoulder. He was glad of her near him, for the princess was broken, and the monstrous girl was turned into a tree, and the frightening girl who threw the country into a daze of sizes, and drove him out of love into the cloudy house, was left alone in the moon's circle and the seven shades behind the screen.

It was hot that morning in the unexpected sunshine. A girl dressed in cotton put her mouth to his ear. 'I'll run you to the sea,' she said, and her breasts jumped up and down as she raced in front of him, with her hair flying wild, to the edge of the sea that was not made of water and the small, thundering pebbles that broke in a million pieces as the dry sea moved in. Along the bright wrackline, from the horizon where the vast birds sailed like boats, from the four compass corners, bellying up through the weed beds, melting from orient and tropic, surging through the ice hills and the whale grounds, through sunset and sunrise corridors, the salt gardens and the herring field, whirlpool and rock pool, out of the trickle in the mountain, down the waterfalls, a white-faced sea of people, the terrible mortal number of the waves, all the centuries' sea drenched in the hail before

Christ, who suffered tomorrow's storm wind, came in with the whole world's voices on the endless beach.

'Come back! Come back!' the boy cried to the girl.

She ran on unheeding over the sand and was lost among the sea. Now her face was a white drop of water in the horizontal rainfall, and her limbs were white as snow and lost in the white, walking tide. Now the heart in her breast was a small red bell that rang in a wave, her colourless hair fringed the spray, and her voice lapped over the flesh-and-bone water.

He cried again, but she had mingled with the people moving in and out. Their tides were drawn by a grave moon that never lost an arc. Their long, sea gestures were deliberate, the flat hands beckoning, the heads uplifted, the eyes in the mask faces set in one direction. Oh, where was she now in the sea? Among the white, walking, and the coral-eyed. 'Come back! Come back! Darling, run out of the sea.' Among the processional waves. The bell in her breast was ringing over the sand.

He ran to the yellow foot of the dunes, calling over his shoulder. 'Run out of the sea.' In the once-green water where the fishes swam, where the gulls rested, where the luminous stones were rubbed and rocked on the scales of the green bed, when ships puffed over the tradeways, and the mad, nameless animals came down to drink the salt. Among the measuring people. Oh, where was she now? The sea was lost behind the dunes. He stumbled on over sand and sandflowers like a blind boy in the sun. The sun dodged round his shoulders.

There was a story once upon a time whispered in the water voice; it blew out the echo from the trees behind the beach in the golden hollows, scraped on the wood until the musical birds and beasts came jumping into sunshine. A raven flew by him, out of a window in the Flood to the blind, wind tower shaking in tomorrow's anger like a scarecrow made out of weathers.

'Once upon a time,' said the water voice.

'Do not adventure any more,' said the echo.

'She is ringing a bell for you in the sea.'

'I am the owl and the echo: you shall never go back.'

On a hill to the horizon stood an old man building a boat, and the light that slanted from the sea cast the holy mountain of a shadow over the three-storied decks and the Eastern timber. And through the sky, out of the beds and gardens, down the white precipice built of feathers, the loud combs and mounds, from the caves in the hill, the cloudy shapes of birds and beasts and insects drifted into the hewn door. A dove with a green petal followed in the raven's flight. Cool rain began to fall.

A Visit to Grandpa's

In the middle of the night I woke from a dream full of whips and lariats as long as serpents, and runaway coaches on mountain passes, and wide, windy gallops over cactus fields, and I heard the man in the next room crying, 'Gee-up!' and 'Whoa!' and trotting his tongue on the roof of his mouth.

It was the first time I had stayed in grandpa's house. The floorboards had squeaked like mice as I climbed into bed, and the mice between the walls had creaked like wood as though another visitor was walking on them. It was a mild summer night, but curtains had flapped and branches beaten against the window. I had pulled the sheet over my head, and soon was roaring and riding in a book.

'Whoa there, my beauties!' cried grandpa. His voice sounded very young and loud, and his tongue had powerful hooves, and he made his bedroom into a great meadow. I thought I would see if he was ill, or had set his bedclothes on fire, for my mother had said that he lit his pipe under the blankets, and had warned me to run to his help if I smelt smoke in the night. I went on tiptoe through the darkness to his bedroom door, brushing against the furniture and upsetting a candlestick with a thump. When I saw there was a light in the room I felt frightened, and as I opened the door I heard grandpa shout, 'Gee-up!' as loudly as a bull with a megaphone.

He was sitting straight up in bed and rocking from side to side as though the bed were on a rough road; the knotted edges of the counterpane were his reins; his invisible horse stood in a shadow beyond the bedside candle. Over a white flannel nightshirt he was wearing a red waistcoat with walnut-sized brass buttons. The over-filled bowl of his pipe smouldered among his whiskers like a little, burning hayrick on a stick. At the sight of me, his hands dropped from the reins and lay blue and quiet, the bed stopped still on a level road, he muffled his tongue into silence, and the horses drew softly up.

'Is there anything the matter, grandpa?' I asked, though the clothes were not on fire. His face in the candlelight looked like a ragged quilt pinned upright on the black air and patched all over with goat-beards.

He stared at me mildly. Then he blew down his pipe, scattering the sparks and making a high, wet dog-whistle of the stem, and shouted: 'Ask no questions.'

After a pause, he said slyly: 'Do you ever have night-mares, boy?'

I said: 'No'

'Oh, yes, you do,' he said.

I said I was woken by a voice that was shouting to horses.

'What did I tell you?' he said 'You eat too much. Who ever heard of horses in a bedroom?'

He fumbled under his pillow, brought out a small tinkling bag, and carefully untied its string. He put a soverign in my hand, and said: 'Buy a cake.' I thanked him and wished him good night.

As I closed my bedroom door, I heard his voice crying loudly and gaily, 'Gee-up! gee-up!' and the rocking of the travelling bed.

In the morning I woke from a dream of fiery horses on a plain that was littered with furniture, and of large, cloudy men who rode six horses at a time and whipped them with burning bed-clothes. Grandpa was at breakfast, dressed in deep black. After breakfast he said, 'There was a terrible loud wind last night,' and sat in his arm-chair by the hearth to make clay balls for the fire. Later in the morning he took me for a walk, through Johnstown village and into the fields on the Llanstephan road.

A man with a whippet said, 'There's a nice morning, Mr Thomas,' and when he had gone, leanly as his dog, into the short-treed green wood he should not have entered because of the notices, grandpa said: 'There, do you hear what he called you? Mister!'

We passed by small cottages, and all the men who leant on the gates congratulated grandpa on the fine morning. We passed through the wood full of pigeons, and their wings broke the branches as they rushed on the tops of the trees. Among the soft, contented voices and the loud, timid flying, grandpa said, like a man calling across a field: 'If you heard those old birds in the night, you'd wake me up and say there were horses in the trees.'

We walked back slowly, for he was tired, and the lean man stalked out of the forbidden wood with a rabbit held as gently over his arm as a girl's arm in a warm sleeve.

On the last day but one of my visit I was taken to Llanstephan in a governess cart pulled by a short, weak pony. Grandpa might have been driving a bison, so tightly he held the reins, so ferociously cracked the long whip, so blasphemously shouted warning to boys who played in the road, so stoutly stood with his gaitered legs apart and cursed the demon strength and wilfulness of the tottering pony.

'Look out, boy!' he cried when we came to each corner, and pulled and tugged and jerked and sweated and waved his whip like a rubber sword. And when the pony had crept miserably round each corner, grandpa turned to me with a sighing smile: 'We weathered that one, boy.'

When we came to Llanstephan village at the top of the hill, he left the cart by the 'Edwinsford Arms' and patted the pony's muzzle and gave it sugar, saying: 'You're a weak little pony, Jim, to pull big men like us.'

He had strong beer and I had lemonade, and he paid Mrs Edwinsford with a sovereign out of the tinkling bag; she inquired after his health, and he said that Llangadock was better for the tubes. We went to look at the churchyard and the sea, and sat in the wood called the Sticks, and stood on the concert platform in the middle of the wood where visitors sang on midsummer nights and, year by year, the innocent of the village was elected mayor. Grandpa paused at the churchyard and pointed over the iron gate at the angelic headstones and the poor wooden crosses. 'There's no sense in lying there,' he said.

We journeyed back furiously: Jim was a bison again.

I woke late on my last morning, out of dreams where the

Llanstephan sea carried bright sailing-boats as long as
liners; and heavenly choirs in the Sticks, dressed in bards'
robes and brass-buttoned waistcoats, sang in a strange
Welsh to the departing sailors. Grandpa was not at
breakfast; he rose early. I walked in the field with a new
sling, and shot at the Towy gulls and the rooks in the
parsonage tree. A warm wind blew from the summer points
of the weather; a morning mist climbed from the ground
and floated among the trees and hid the noisy birds; in the
mist and the wind my pebbles flew lightly up like hailstones
in a world on its head. The morning passed without a bird
falling.

I broke my sling and returned for the midday meal
through the parson's orchard, Once, grandpa told me, the
parson had bought three ducks at Carmarthen Fair and
made a pond for them in the centre of the garden, but they
waddled to the gutter under the crumbling doorsteps of the
house, and swam and quacked there. When I reached the
end of the orchard path, I looked through a hole in the
hedge and saw that the parson had made a tunnel through
the rockery that was between the gutter and the pond and
had set up a notice in plain writing: 'This way to the pond.'

The ducks were still swimming under the steps.

Grandpa was not in the cottage. I went into the garden,
but grandpa was not staring at the fruit-trees. I called across
to a man who leant on a spade in the field beyond the garden
hedge: 'Have you seen my grandpa this morning?'

He did not stop digging, and answered over his shoulder:
'I seen him in his fancy waistcoat.'

Griff, the barber, lived in the next cottage. I called to him
through the open door: 'Mr Griff, have you seen my
grandpa?'

The barber came out in his shirtsleeves.

I said: 'He's wearing his best waistcoat.' I did not know if
it was important, but grandpa wore his waistcoat only in
the night.

'Has grandpa been to Llanstephan?' asked Mr Griff
anxiously.

'He went there yesterday in a little trap,' I said.

He hurried indoors and I heard him talking in Welsh, and he came out again with his white coat on, and he carried a striped and coloured walking-stick. He strode down the village street and I ran by his side.

When we stopped at the tailor's shop, he cried out, 'Dan!' and Dan Tailor stepped from his window where he sat like an Indian priest but wearing a derby hat. 'Dai Thomas has got his waistcoat on,' said Mr Griff, 'and he's been to Llanstephan.'

As Dan Tailor searched for his overcoat, Mr Griff was striding on. 'Will Evans,' he called outside the carpenter's shop, 'Dai Thomas has been to Llanstephan, and he's got his waistcoat on.'

'I'll tell Morgan now,' said the carpenter's wife out of the hammering, sawing darkness of the shop.

We called at the butcher's shop and Mr Price's house, and Mr Griff repeated his message like a town crier.

We gathered together in Johnstown square. Dan Tailor had his bicycle, Mr Price his pony trap. Mr Griff, the butcher, Morgan carpenter, and I climbed into the shaking trap, and we trotted off towards Carmarthen town. The tailor led the way, ringing his bell as though there were a fire or a robbery, and an old woman by the gate of a cottage at the end of the street ran inside like a pelted hen. Another woman waved a bright handkerchief.

'Where are we going?' I asked.

Grandpa's neighbours were as solemn as old men with black hats and jackets on the outskirts of a fair. Mr Griff shook his head and mourned: 'I didn't expect this again from Dai Thomas.'

'Not after last time,' said Mr Price sadly.

We trotted on, we crept up Constitution Hill, we rattled down into Lammas Street, and the tailor still rang his bell and a dog ran, squealing, in front of his wheels. As we clip-clopped over the cobbles that led down to the Towy bridge, I remembered grandpa's nightly noisy journeys that rocked the bed and shook the walls, and I saw his gay waistcoat in a vision and his patchwork head tufted and smiling in the candlelight. The tailor before us turned round on his saddle, his bicycle wobbled and skidded. 'I see Dai Thomas!' he cried.

The trap rattled on to the bridge, and I saw grandpa there: the buttons of his waistcoat shone in the sun, he wore his tight, black Sunday trousers and a tall, dusty hat I had seen in a cupboard in the attic, and he carried an ancient bag. He bowed to us. 'Good morning, Mr Price,' he said, 'and Mr Griff and Mr Morgan and Mr Evans.' To me he said: 'Good morning, boy.'

Mr Griff pointed his coloured stick at him.

'And what do you think you are doing on Carmarthen bridge in the middle of the afternoon,' he said sternly, 'with your best waistcoat and your old hat?'

Grandpa did not answer, but inclined his face to the river wind, so that his beard was set dancing and wagging as though he talked, and watched the coracle men move, like turtles, on the shore.

Mr Griff raised his stunted barber's pole. 'And where do you think you are going,' he said, 'with your old black bag?'

Grandpa said: 'I am going to Llangadock to be buried.' And he watched the coracle shells slip into the water lightly, and the gulls complain over the fish-filled water as bitterly as Mr Price complained:

'But you aren't dead yet, Dai Thomas.'

For a moment grandpa reflected, then: 'There's no sense in lying dead in Llanstephan,' he said. 'The ground is comfy in Llangadock; you can twitch your legs without putting them in the sea.'

His neighbours moved close to him. They said: 'You aren't dead, Mr Thomas.'

'How can you be buried, then?'

'Nobody's going to bury you in Llanstephan.'

'Come on home, Mr Thomas.'

'There's strong beer for tea.'

'And cake.'

But grandpa stood firmly on the bridge, and clutched his bag to his side, and stared at the flowing river and the sky, like a prophet who has no doubt.

Who Do You Wish Was With Us?

Birds in the Crescent trees were singing; boys on bicycles were ringing their bells and pedalling down the slight slope to make the whirrers in their wheels startle the women gabbing on the sunny doorsteps; small girls on the pavement, wheeling young brothers and sisters in prams, were dressed in their summer best and with coloured ribbons; on the circular swing in the public playground, children from the snot school spun themselves happy and sick, crying 'Swing us!' and 'Swing us!' and 'Ooh! I'm falling!'; the morning was as varied and bright as though it were an international or a jubilee when Raymond Price and I, flannelled and hatless, with sticks and haversacks, set out together to walk to the Worm's Head. Striding along, in step, through the square of the residential Uplands, we brushed by young men in knife-creased whites and showing-off blazers, and hockey-legged girls with towels round their necks and celluloid sun-glasses, and struck a letterbox with our sticks, and bullied our way through a crowd of day-trippers who waited at the stop of the Gower-bound buses, and stepped over luncheon baskets, not caring if we trod in them.

'Why can't those bus lizards walk?' Ray said.

'They were born too tired,' I said.

We went on up Sketty Road at a great speed, our haversacks jumping on our backs. We rapped on every gate to give a terrific walker's benediction to the people in the choking houses. Like a breath of fresh air we passed a man in office pin-stripes standing, with a dog-lead in his hand, whistling at a corner. Tossing the sounds and smells of the town from us with the swing of our shoulders and loose-limbed strides, half-way up the road we heard women on an outing call 'Mutt and Jeff!' for Ray was tall and thin and I was short. Streamers flew out of the charabanc. Ray, sucking hard at his bulldog pipe, walked too fast to wave and did not even smile. I wondered whom I had missed among the waving women bowling over the rise. My love to come, with a paper cap on, might have sat at the back of the outing, next to the barrel; but, once away from the familiar roads and swinging towards the coast, I forgot her face and voice, that had been made at night, and breathed the country air in.

'There's a different air here. You breathe. It's like the country,' Ray said, 'and a bit of the sea mixed. Draw it down; it'll blow off the nicotine.'

He spat in his hand. 'Still town grey,' he said.

He put back the spit in his mouth and we walked on with our heads high.

By this time we were three miles from the town. The semi-detached houses, with a tin-roofed garage each and a kennel in the back plot and a mowed lawn, with sometimes a hanging coco-nut on a pole, or a bird-bath, or a bush like a peacock, grew fewer when we reached the outskirts of the common.

Ray stopped and sighed and said: 'Wait half a sec, I want to fill the old pipe.' He held a match to it as though we were in a storm.

Hotfaced and wet-browed, we grinned at each other. Already the day had brought us close as truants; we were running away, or walking with pride and mischief, arrogantly from the streets that owned us into the unpredictable country. I thought it was again our fate to stride in the sun without the shop-windows dazzling or the music of mowers rising above the birds. A bird's dropping fell on a fence. It was one in the eye for the town. A sheep cried 'Baa!' out of sight, and that would show the Uplands. I did not know what it would show. 'A couple of wanderers in wild Wales,' Ray said, winking, and a lorry carrying cement drove past us towards the golf links. He slapped my haversack and straightened his shoulders. 'Come on, Let's be going.' We walked uphill faster than before.

A party of cyclists had pulled up on the roadside and were drinking dandelion and burdock from paper cups. I saw the empty bottles in a bush. All the boys wore singlets and shorts, and the girls wore open cricket shirts and boy's long grey trousers, with safety-pins for clips at the bottoms.

'There's room for one behind, sonny boy,' a girl on a tandem said to me.

'It won't be a stylish marriage,' Ray said.

'That was quick,' I told Ray as we walked away from them and the boys began to sing.

'God, I like this!' said Ray. On the first rise of the dusty road through the spreading heathered common, he shaded his eyes and looked all round him, smoking like a chimney and pointing with his Irish stick at the distant clumps of trees and sights of the sea between them. 'Down there is Oxwich, but you can't see it. That's a farm. See the roof? No, there, follow my finger. This is the life,' he said.

Side by side, thrashing the low banks, we marched down the very middle of the road, and Ray saw a rabbit running. 'You wouldn't think this was near town. It's wild.'

We pointed out the birds whose names we knew, and the rest of the names we made up. I saw gulls and crows, though the crows may have been rooks, and Ray said that thrushes and swallows and skylarks flew above us as we hurried and hummed.

He stopped to pull some blades of grass. 'They should be straws,' he said, and put them in his mouth next to his pipe. 'God, the sky's blue! Think of me, in the G.W.R. when all this is about. Rabbits and fields and farms. You wouldn't think I'd suffered to look at me now. I could do anything, I could drive cows, I could plough a field.'

His father and sister and brother were dead, and his mother sat all day in a wheel-chair, crippled with arthritis. He was ten years older than I was. He had a lined and bony face and a tight, crooked mouth. His upper lip had vanished.

Alone on the long road, the common in the heat mist wasting for miles on either side, we walked on under the afternoon sun, growing thirsty and drowsy but never slowing our pace. Soon the cycling party rode by, three boys and three girls and the one girl on the tandem, all laughing and ringing.

'How's Shanks's pony?'

'We'll see you on the way back.'

'You'll be walking still.'

'Like a crutch?' they shouted.

Then they were gone. The dust settled again. Their bells rang faintly through the wood around the road before us. The wild common, six miles and a bit from the town, lay back without a figure on it, and, under the trees, smoking hard to keep the gnats away, we leant against a trunk and talked like men, on the edge of an untrodden place, who have not seen another man for years.

'Do you remember Curly Parry?'

I had seen him only two days ago in the snooker-room, but his dimpled face was fading, even as I thought of him, into the colours of our walk, the ash-white of the road, the common heathers, the green and blue of fields and fragmentary sea, and the memory of his silly voice was lost in the sounds of birds and unreasonably moving leaves in the lack of wind.

'I wonder what he's doing now? He should get out more in the open air, he's a proper town boy. Look at us here.' Ray waved his pipe at the trees and leafy sky. 'I wouldn't change this for High Street.'

I looked at us there; a boy and a young man, with faces, under the strange sunburn, pale from the cramped town, out of breath and hot-footed, pausing in the early afternoon on a road through a popular wood, and I could see the unaccustomed happiness in Ray's eyes and the impossible friendliness in mine, and Ray protested against his history each time he wondered or pointed in the country scene and I had more love in me than I could ever want or use.

'Yes, look at us here,' I said, 'dawdling about. Worm's Head is twelve miles off. Don't you want to hear a tramcar, Ray? That's a wood pigeon. See! The boys are out on the streets with the sports special now. Paper! paper! I bet you Curl's potting the red. Come on! come on!'

'Eyes right!' said Ray, 'I's b——d! Remember that story?'

Up the road and out of the wood, and a double-decker roared behind us.

'The Rhossilli bus is coming,' I said.

We both held up our sticks to stop it.

'Why did you stop the bus?' Ray said, when we were sitting upstairs. 'This was a walking holiday.'

'You stopped it as well.'

We sat in front like two more drivers.

'Can't you mind the ruts?' I said.

'You're wobbling,' said Ray.

We opened our haversacks and shared the sandwiches and hard-boiled eggs and meat paste and drank from the thermos in turns.

'When we get home don't say we took a bus,' I said. 'Pretend we walked all day. There goes Oxwich! It doesn't seem far, does it? We'd have had beards by now.'

The bus passed the cyclists crawling up a hill. 'Like a tow along?' I shouted, but they couldn't hear. The girl on the tandem was a long way behind the others.

We sat with our lunch on our laps, forgetting to steer, letting the driver in his box beneath drive where and how he liked on the switch-back road, and saw grey chapels and weather-worn angels; at the feet of the hills farthest from the sea, pretty, pink cottages – horrible, I thought, to live in, for grass and trees would imprison me more securely than any jungle of packed and swarming streets and chimney-roosting roofs – and petrol pumps and hayricks and a man on a cart-horse standing stock still in a ditch, surrounded by flies.

'This is the way to see the country.'

The bus, on a narrow hill, sent two haversacked walkers bounding to the shelter of the hedge, where they stretched out their arms and drew their bellies in.

'That might have been you and me.'

We looked back happily at the men against the hedge. They climbed on to the road, slow as snails continued walking, and grew smaller.

At the entrance to Rhossilli we pushed the conductor's bell and stopped the bus, and walked, with springing steps, the few hundred yards to the village.

'We've done it in pretty good time,' said Ray.

'I think it's a record,' I said.

Laughing on the cliff above the very long golden beach, we pointed out to each other, as though the other were blind, the great rock of the Worm's Head. The sea was out. We crossed over on slipping stones and stood, at last, triumphantly on the windy top. There was monstrous, thick grass there that made us spring-heeled, and we laughed and bounced on it, scaring the sheep who ran up and down the battered sides like goats. Even on this calmest day a wind blew along the Worm. At the end of the humped and serpentine body, more gulls than I had ever seen before cried over their new dead and the droppings of ages. On the point, the sound of my quiet voice was scooped and magnified into a hollow shout, as though the wind around me had made a shell or cave, with blue, intangible roof and sides, as tall and wide as all the arched sky, and the flapping gulls were made thunderous. Standing there, legs apart, one hand on my hip, shading my eyes like Raleigh in some picture, I thought myself alone in the epileptic moment near bad sleep, when the legs grow long and sprout into the night and the heart hammers to wake the neighbours and breath is a hurricane through the elastic room. Instead of becoming small on the great rock poised between sky and sea, I felt myself the size of a breathing building, and only Ray in the world could match my lovely bellow as I said: 'Why don't we live here always? Always and always. Build a bloody house and live like bloody kings!' The word bellowed among the squawking birds, they carried it off to the headland in the drums of their wings; like a tower, Ray pranced on the unsteady edge of a separate rock and beat about with his stick, which could turn into snakes or flames; and we sank to the ground, the rubbery, gull-limed grass, the sheep-pilled stones, the pieces of bones and feathers, and crouched at the extreme point of the Peninsula. We were still for so long that the dirty-grey gulls calmed down, and some settled near us.

Then we finished our food.

'This isn't like any other place,' I said. I was almost my own size again, five feet five and eight stone, and my voice didn't sweep any longer up to the amplifying sky. 'It could be in the middle of the sea. You could think the Worm was moving, couldn't you? Guide it to Ireland, Ray. We'll see W. B. Yeats and you can kiss the Blarney. We'll have a fight in Belfast.'

Ray looked out of place on the end of the rock. He would not make himself easy and loll in the sun and roll on to his side to stare down a precipice into the sea, but tried to sit upright as though he were in a hard chair and had nothing to do with his hands. He fiddled with his tame stick and waited for the day to be orderly, for the Head to grow paths and for railings to shoot up on the scarred edges.

'It's too wild for a townee,' I said.

'Townee yourself! Who stopped the bus?'

'Aren't you glad we stopped it? We'd still be walking, like Felix. You're just pretending you don't like it here. You were dancing on the edge.'

'Only a couple of hops.'

'I know what it is, you don't like the furniture. There's not enough sofas and chairs,' I said.

'You think you're a country boy; you don't know a cow from a horse.'

We began to quarrel, and soon Ray felt at home again and forgot the monotonous out-of-doors. If snow had fallen suddenly he would not have noticed. He drew down into himself, and the rock, to him, became dark as a house with the blinds drawn. The sky-house shapes that had danced and bellowed at birds crept down to hide, two small town mutterers in a hollow.

I knew what was going to happen by the way Ray lowered his head and brought his shoulders up so that he looked like a man with no neck, and by the way he sucked his breath in between his teeth. He stared at his dusty white shoes and I knew what shapes his imagination made of them; they were the feet of a man dead in bed, and he was going to talk about his brother. Sometimes, leaning against a fence when we watched football, I caught him staring at his own thin hand; he was thinning it more and more, removing the flesh, seeing Harry's hand in front of him, with the bones appearing through the sensitive skin. If he lost the world around him for a moment, if I left him alone, if he cast his eyes down, if his hand lost its grip on the hard, real fence or the hot bowl of his pipe, he would be back in ghastly bedrooms, carrying cloths and basins and listening for handbells.

'I've never seen such a lot of gulls,' I said. 'Have you ever seen such a lot? Such a lot of gulls. You try and count them. Two of them are fighting up there; look, pecking each other like hens in the air. What'll you bet the big one wins? Old dirty beak! I wouldn't like to have had his dinner, a bit of sheep and dead gull.' I swore at myself for saying the word 'dead.' 'Wasn't it gay in town this morning?' I said.

Ray stared at his hand. Nothing could stop him now. 'Wasn't it gay in town this morning? Everybody laughing and smiling in their summer outfits. The kids were playing and everybody was happy; they almost had the band out. I used to hold my father down on the bed when he had fits. I had to change the sheets twice a day for my brother, there was blood on everything. I watched him getting thinner and thinner; in the end you could lift him up with one hand. And his wife wouldn't go to see him because he coughed in her face, Mother couldn't move, and I had to cook as well, cook and nurse and change the sheets and hold father down when he got mad. It's embittered my outlook,' he said.

'But you loved the walk, you enjoyed yourself on the common. It's a wonderful day, Ray. I'm sorry about your brother. Let's explore. Let's climb down to the sea. Perhaps there's a cave with prehistoric drawings, and we can write an article and make a fortune. Let's climb down.'

'My brother used to ring a bell for me; he could only whisper. He used to say: "Ray, look at my legs. Are they thinner to-day?"'

'The sun's going down. Let's climb.'

'Father thought I was trying to murder him when I held him on the bed. I was holding him down when he died, and he rattled. Mother was in the kitchen in her chair, but she knew he was dead and she started screaming for my sister. Brenda was in a sanatorium in Craigynos. Harry rang the bell in his bedroom when mother started, but I couldn't go to him, and father was dead in the bed.'

'I'm going to climb to the sea,' I said. 'Are you coming?'

He got up out of the hollow into the open world again and followed me slowly over the point and down the steep side; the gulls rose in a storm. I clung to dry, spiked bushes but the roots came out; a foothold crumbled, a crevice for the fighters broke as I groped in it; I scrambled on to a black, flat-backed rock whose head, like a little Worm's, curved out of the sea a few perilous steps away from me, and, drenched by flying water, I gazed up to see Ray and a shower of stones falling. He landed at my side.

'I thought I was done for,' he said, when he had stopped shaking. 'I could see all my past life in a flash.'

'All of it?'

'Well, nearly. I saw my brother's face clear as yours.'

We watched the sun set.

'Like an orange.'

'Like a tomato.'

'Like a goldfish bowl.'

We went one better than the other, describing the sun. The sea beat on our rock, soaked our trouser-legs, stung our cheeks. I took off my shoes and held Ray's hand and slid down the rock on my belly to trail my feet in the sea. Then Ray slid down, and I held him fast while he kicked up water.

'Come back now,' I said, pulling his hand.

'No, no,' he said, 'this is delicious. Let me keep my feet in a bit more. It's warm as the baths.' He kicked and grunted and slapped the rock in a frenzy with his other hand, pretending to drown. 'Don't save me!' he cried. 'I'm drowning! I'm drowning!'

I pulled him back, and in his struggles he brushed a shoe off the rock. We fished it out. It was full of water.

'Never mind, it was worth it. I haven't paddled since I was six. I can't tell you how much I enjoyed it.'

He had forgotten about his father and his brother, but I knew that once his joy in the wild, warm water was over he would return to the painful house and see his brother growing thinner. I had heard Harry die so many times, and the mad father was as familiar to me as Ray himself. I knew every cough and cry, every clawing at the air.

'I'm going to paddle once a day from now on,' Ray said. 'I'm going to go down to the sands every evening and have a good paddle. I'm going to splash about and get wet up to my knees. I don't care who laughs.'

He sat still for a minute, thinking gravely of this. 'When I wake up in the mornings there's nothing to look forward to, except on Saturdays,' he said then, 'or when I come up to your house for Lexicon. I may as well be dead. But now I'll be able to wake up and think: "This evening I'm going to splash about in the sea." I'm going to do it again now.' He rolled up his wet trousers and slid down the rock. 'Don't let go.'

As he kicked his legs in the sea, I said: 'This is a rock at the world's end. We're all alone. It all belongs to us, Ray. We can have anybody we like here and keep everybody else away. Who do you wish was with us?'

He was too busy to answer, splashing and snorting, blowing as though his head were under, making circular commotions in the water or lazily skimming the surface with his toes.

'Who would you like to be here on the rock with us?'

He was stretched out like a dead man, his feet motionless in the sea, his mouth on the rim of a rock pool, his hand clutched round my foot.

'I wish George Gray was with us,' I said. 'He's the man from London who's come to live in Norfolk Street. You don't know him. He's the most curious man I ever met, queerer than Oscar Thomas, and I thought nobody could ever be queerer than that. George Gray wears glasses, but there's no glass in them, only the frames. You wouldn't know until you came near him. He does all sorts of things. He's a cat's doctor and he goes to somewhere in Sketty every morning to help a woman put her clothes on. She's an old widow, he said, and she can't dress by herself. I don't know how he came to know her. He's only been in town for a month. He's a B.A., too. The things he's got in his pockets! Pincers, and scissors for cats, and lots of diaries. He read me some of the diaries, about the jobs he did in London. He used to go to bed with a policewoman and she used to pay him. She used to go to bed in her uniform. I've never met such a queer man. I wish he was here now. Who do you wish was with us, Ray?'

Ray began to move his feet again, kicking them out straight behind him and bringing them down hard on the water, and then stirring the water about.

'I wish Gwilym was here, too,' I said. 'I've told you about him. He could give a sermon to the sea. This is the very place, there isn't anywhere as lonely as this.' Oh, the beloved sunset! Oh, the terrible sea! Pity the sailors, pity the sinners, pity Raymond Price and me! Oh, the evening is coming like a cloud! Amen. Amen. 'Who do you wish, Ray?'

'I wish my brother was with us,' Ray said. He climbed on to the flat of the rock and dried his feet. 'I wish Harry was here. I wish he was here now, at this moment, on this rock.'

The sun was nearly right down, halved by the shadowed sea. Cold came up, spraying out of the sea, and I could make a body for it, icy antlers, a dripping tail, a rippling face with fishes passing across it. A wind, cornering the Head, chilled through our summer shirts, and the sea began to cover our rock quickly, our rock already covered with friends, with living and dead, racing against the darkness. We did not speak as we climbed. I thought: 'If we open our mouths we'll both say: "Too late, it's too late."' We ran over the spring-board grass and the scraping rock needles, down the hollow in which Ray had talked about blood, up rustling humps, and along the ragged flat. We stood on the beginning of the Head and looked down, though both of us could have said, without looking: 'The sea is in.'

The sea was in. The slipping stepping-stones were gone.

On the mainland, in the dusk, some little figures beckoned to us. Seven clear figures, jumping and calling. I thought they were the cyclists.

The Crumbs of One Man's Year

Slung as though in a hammock, or a lull, between one Christmas for ever over and a New Year nearing full of relentless surprises, waywardly and gladly I pry back at those wizening twelve months and see only a waltzing snippet of the tipsy-turvy times, flickers of vistas, flashes of queer fishes, patches and chequers of a bard's-eye view.

Of what is coming in the New Year I know nothing, except that all that is certain will come like thunderclaps or like comets in the shape of four-leaved clovers, and that all that is unforeseen will appear with the certainty of the sun who every morning shakes a leg in the sky; and of what has gone I know only shilly-shally snatches and freckled plaids, flecks and dabs, dazzle and froth; a simple second caught in coursing snow-light, an instant, gay or sorry, struck motionless in the curve of flight like a bird or a scythe; the spindrift leaf and stray-paper whirl, canter, quarrel, and people-chase of everybody's street; suddenly the way the grotesque wind slashes and freezes at a corner the clothes of a passer-by so that she stays remembered, cold and still until the world like a night-light in a nursery goes out; and a waddling couple of the small occurrences, comic as ducks, that quack their way through our calamitous days; whits and dots and tittles.

'Look back, back,' the big voices clarion, 'look back at the black colossal year,' while the rich music fanfares and dead-marches.

I can give you only a scattering of some of the crumbs of one man's year; and the penny music whistles.

Any memory, of the long, revolving year, will do, to begin with.

I was walking, one afternoon in August, along a river-bank, thinking the same thoughts that I always think when I walk along a river-bank in August. As I was walking, I was thinking – now it is August and I am walking along a river-bank. I do not think I was thinking of anything else. I should have been thinking of what I should have been doing, but I was thinking only of what I was doing then and it was all right: it was good, and ordinary, and slow, and idle, and old, and sure, and what I was doing I could have been doing a thousand years before, had I been alive then and myself or any other man. You could have thought the river was ringing – almost you could hear the green, rapid bells sing in it: it could have been the River Elusina, 'that dances at the noise of Musick, for with Musick it bubbles, dances and growes sandy, and so continues till the musick ceases . . .' or it could have been the river 'in Judea that runs swiftly all the six dayes of the week, and stands still and rests all their Sabbath.' There were trees blowing, standing still, growing, knowing, whose names I never knew. (Once, indeed, with a friend I wrote a poem beginning, 'All trees are oaks, except fir-trees.') There were birds being busy, or sleep-flying, in the sky. (The poem had continued: 'All birds are robins, except crows, or rooks.') Nature was doing what it was doing, and thinking just that. And I was walking and thinking that I was walking, and for August it was not such a cold day. And then I saw, drifting along the water, a piece of paper, and I thought: Something wonderful may be written on this paper. I was alone on the gooseberry earth, or alone for two green miles, and a message drifted towards me on that tabby-coloured water that ran through the middle of the cow-patched, mooing fields. It was a message from multitudinous nowhere to my solitary self. I put out my stick and caught the piece of paper and held it close to the river-bank. It was a page torn from a very old periodical. That I could see. I leant over and read, through water, the message on the rippling page. I made out, with difficulty, only one sentence: it commemorated the fact that, over a hundred years ago, a man in Worcester had, for a bet, eaten, at one sitting, fifty-two pounds of plums.

And any other memory, of the long evolving year, will do, to go on with.

Here now, to my memory, come peaceful blitz and pieces of the Fifth of November, guys in the streets and forks in the sky, when Catherine-wheels and Jacky-jumps and good bombs burst in the blistered areas. The rockets are few but they star between roofs and up to the wall of the warless night. 'A penny for the Guy?' 'No, that's my father.' The great joke brocks and sizzles. Sirius explodes in the backyard by the shelter. Timorous ladies sit in their backrooms, with the eighth programme on very loud. Retiring men snarl under their blankets. In the unkempt-gardens of the very rich, the second butler lights a squib. In everybody's street the fearless children shout, under the little homely raids. But I was standing on a signalling country hill where they fed a hungry bonfire Guy with brushwood, sticks, and crackerjacks; the bonfire Guy whooped for more; small sulphurous puddings banged in his burning belly, and his thorned hair caught. He lurched, and made common noises. He was a long time dying on the hill over the starlit fields where the tabby river, without a message, ran on, with bells and trout and tins and bangles and literature and cats in it, to the sea never out of sound.

And on one occasion, in this long dissolving year, I remember that I boarded a London bus from a district I have forgotten, and where I certainly could have been up to little good, to an appointment that I did not want to keep.

It was a shooting green spring morning, nimble and crocus, with all the young women treading on naked flower-stalks, the metropolitan sward, swinging their milkpail handbags, gentle, fickle, inviting, accessible, forgiving each robustly abandoned gesture of salutation before it was made or imagined, assenting, as they revelled demurely towards the manicure *salon* or the typewriting office, to all the ardent unspoken endearments of shaggy strangers and the winks and pipes of clovenfooted sandwichmen. The sun shrilled, the buses gambolled, policemen and daffodils bowed in the breeze that tasted of buttermilk. Delicate carousal splashed and babbled from the public-houses which were not yet open. I felt like a young god. I removed my collar-studs and opened my shirt. I tossed back my hair. There was an aviary in my heart, but without any owls or eagles. My cheeks were cherried warm, I smelt, I thought, of sea-pinks. To the sound of madrigals sung by slim sopranos in waterfalled valleys where I was the only tenor, I leapt on to a bus. The bus was full. Carefree, open-collared, my eyes alight, my veins full of the spring as a dancer's shoes should be full of champagne, I stood, in love and at ease and always young, on the packed lower deck. And a man exactly my own age – or perhaps he was a little older – got up and offered me his seat. He said, in a respectful voice, as though to an old justice of the peace, 'Please, won't you take my seat?' and then he added – 'Sir.'

How many variegations of inconsiderable defeats and disillusionments I have forgotten! How many shades and shapes from the polychromatic zebra house! How many Joseph-coats I have left uncalled-for in the Gentlemen's Cloakrooms of the year!

And one man's year is like the country of a cloud, mapped on the sky, that soon will vanish into the watery, ordered wastes, into the spinning rule, into the dark which is light. Now the cloud is flying, very slowly, out of sight, and I can remember of all that voyaging geography, no palaced morning hills or huge plush valleys in the downing sun, forests simmering with birds, stagged moors, merry legendary meadowland, bullish plains, but only – the street near Waterloo station where a small boy, wearing cut-down khaki and a steel helmet, pushed a pram full of firewood and shouted, in a dispassionate voice, after each passer-by: 'Where's your tail?'

The estuary pool under the collapsed castle, where the July children rolled together in original mud, shrieking and yawping, and low life, long before newts, twitched on their hands.

The crisp path through the field in this December snow, in the deep dark, where we trod the buried grass like ghosts on dry toast.

The single-line run along the spring-green river-bank where water-voles went Indian file to work, and where the young impatient voles, in their sleek vests, always in a hurry, jumped over the threadbare backs of the old ones.

The razor-scarred back-street café bar where a man with cut cheeks and chewed ears, huskily and furiously complained, over tarry tea, that the new baby panda in the zoo was not floodlit.

The gully sands in March, under the flayed and flailing cliff-top trees, when the wind played old Harry, or old Thomas, with me, and cormorants, far off, sped like motor-boats across the bay, as I weaved towards the toppling town and the black, loud *Lion* where the cat, who purred like a fire, looked out of two cinders at the gently swilling retired sea-captains in the snug-as-a-bug back bar.

And the basement kitchen in nipping February, with napkins on the line slung across from door to chockablock corner, and a bicycle by the larder very much down at wheels, and hats and toy-engines and bottles and spanners on the broken rocking-chair, and billowing papers and half-finished crosswords stacked on the radio always turned full tilt, and the fire smoking, and onions peeling, and chips always spitting on the stove, and small men in their overcoats talking of self-discipline and the ascetic life until the air grew woodbine-blue and the clock choked and the traffic died.

And then the moment of a night in that cavorting spring, rare and unforgettable as a bicycle-clip found in the middle of the desert. The lane was long and soused and dark that led to the house I helped to fill and bedraggle.

'Who's left this in the corner?'

'What, where?'

'Here, this.'

A doll's arm, the chitterlings of a clock, a saucepan full of hatbands.

The lane was rutted as though by bosky watercarts, and so dark you couldn't see your front in spite of you. Rain barrelled down. On one side you couldn't hear the deer that lived there, and on the other side – voices began to whisper, muffled in the midnight sack. A man's voice and a woman's voice. 'Lovers,' I said to myself. For at night the heart comes out, like a cat on the tiles. Discourteously I shone my torch.

There, in the thick rain, a young man and a young woman stood, very close together, near the hedge that whirred in the wind. And a yard from them, another young man sat staidly, on the grass verge, holding an open book from which he appeared to read. And in the very rutted and puddly middle of the lane, two dogs were fighting, with brutish concentration and in absolute silence.

INDEX OF TITLES AND FIRST LINES

Titles of poems in italics; titles of prose works in capitals. Where the first line of a poem is the same as the title, it is not repeated.